WESTERN

SAM HOOK

Also by Richard S. Wheeler
In Thorndike Large Print

Winter Grass

SAM HOOK

Richard S. Wheeler

Thorndike Press • Thorndike, Maine

Library of Congress Cataloging in Publication Data:

Wheeler, Richard S.
  Sam Hook.
  1. Large type books. I. Title.
[PS3573.H4345S3   1987]   813'.54   87-9989
ISBN 0-89621-809-0 (lg. print: alk. paper)

All the characters and events portrayed in this story are fictitious.

Large Print edition available in North America by arrangement with Walker & Company.

Cover design by James B. Murray.

To Jory and Charlotte Sherman

CHAPTER 1

Sam Hook is a stubborn old man. I knew he was coming for me the moment I spotted him out there, rain dripping off his bent hat brim, tying his ugly horse.

That was like him. Ride twenty miles in an icy spring rain for some fool principle or other. Them kind never get along in life.

He stomped in, rain spraying off his slicker with every step, and glared at me. I wasn't happy to see him — and I sure didn't want to go out in that drizzle, whatever his problem might be.

"Hello, Will," he piped with a reedy voice that seemed to rise out of his white mustache. "I've a problem you're about to solve."

He hung the slicker on a peg and settled down across from my solitaire game, which was going nicely because I had bent the rules.

"Ten bulls shot," he announced, dumping half a dozen mangled slugs on my desk. He stared at me through those rheumy hazel eyes, making me uncomfortable.

"Felony," he said. "Get your duds and we'll ride out. Rain washed the prints away, but you'd better have a look."

I knew it. "No rush," I grumbled. "Nothing I can do about it anyway."

"You can get your fat fanny on a wet saddle and look before the vultures eat the evidence," Hook retorted.

"Forty-four forties, looks like," I said. "Some evidence."

"Well?" The old man drew himself up in the wooden chair.

"Your problem, not mine. You've been asking for it."

A look of disgust crept over his face, and that riled me some.

"Property deliberately destroyed. A lot more of my bulls in danger. Law broken. And you're telling me you're going to sit there and do nothing. Your butt gets fatter every year, Oglesby."

"You don't catch flies with vinegar," I replied.

He glared at me. I had experienced that glare before and hated it. He'd lock his unblinking eyes on mine, just waiting until I'd be forced to turn away.

"I'll just wait here until you think it out," he said quietly, settling back. The old boy was thin as a posthole, but he had some infernal way of filling a whole room.

"Red jack goes on the black queen," he said. "Then you get to see the card underneath."

" 'Nother red jack," I said.

He smiled darkly at me. Stubborn old codger.

"The way I see it," I said finally, "it's a private matter between you and the Association. You're standing in the way of progress, they figger, with your scroungy longhorns. Now looks like they're riled up, killing them scrub bulls of yours. All you had to do was go along. Them Herefords got more meat and get a better price anyway. Was I the Association, I'd be riled too, getting them purebreds bred by your scruffy Texas beeves all the time."

Hook's eyes glinted. "Are you telling me, Oglesby, there's a law outlawing longhorns on public range?"

"Well, hell, Sam, you know —"

"What I know is that my beeves have a right to be there, and that a crime's been committed, and that you intend to do nothing about it."

Actually, this had been going on for two years. The rest of the ranchers all switched over after the bad winter of eighty-six down there along the Smith and Shields Rivers. Meagher County was Hereford country, all except for old

Hook, and I don't like riling up voting folks if I can help it. Eighteen of them ranches were Hereford or Angus. Hook was the holdout, doing things exactly the way he had always done them since he arrived down there in seventy-two and patented his home section and a few forties around springs. All the ranchers were using public range.

"Deputize me," he said.

"Huh?"

"You heard me. Deputize me."

"I can't —"

"Of course you will." His rheumy eyes were nailing me again.

"You're an old man, Sam. You can't be arresting the likes of Hamilton Bark."

He never blinked. "Write it out properly and swear me in."

Well, I thought, maybe deputizing the old fogey had its uses. Then he'd be under my command. And I'd save a trip in the rain. I shrugged, and scratched out the commission. The nib on that steel pen was plumb wore out because the county was so cheap, and I had to blot up the mess.

"Raise your hand," I said. "You solemnly swear to uphold the law of Meagher County, Montana Territory?"

"Do."

"Here's your star."

He pinned it to the inside of his sheepskin vest.

"Save you a trip in the rain," he said, grinning, as he shrugged into his slicker.

The door latched quietly behind him.

Stubborn old Hook, I thought. I heard hoofbeats slopping away. Seventy years old, likely. Lotta fun he'd have arresting those he-coons down there. Still, the old boy had grit. And that double-barreled sawed-off scattergun. I never did see him with a six-gun, but that old two-holer was something for anyone in his right mind to respect. I'd seen men cut in two with those. And you didn't have to aim them, neither.

I peered out the watery window, watching him slop down the street as if it was some sunny day in White Sulphur Springs. Off to Maud's, east of town, for certain. He had some kind of lash-up with her, though I never figgered just what. That kid at the bank, wanting to shine up to the star I'm wearing, whispered to me that Maud Wall deposited a sixty-dollar draft from old Hook regular as clockwork each month, as if she was his kept woman or something.

But she wasn't. Leastwise I didn't figger she was. She was too plain, and in any case, he was too old. And besides, her setup out there was respectable, far as that goes. She ran one of them places – there ain't no name for them but everybody knows of them – where girls in trouble go and hide out. Maud, I knew she was a midwife, but I never found out much else about her, though I've suspicioned she was on the lam from the law, or maybe from a bad husband. But nothing I could nail down.

Anyway, she ran that house out there, and most everybody in central Montana knew of it. Girl'd get diddled by some cowhand and she'd end up there, and he'd send Maud twenty-five out of his thirty-and-found for the time. And she'd deliver the girl, or get Doc Easum if she needed help.

Only time I ever was in there was when a girl died birthing and I had to make a report. Nice place inside, all clean, with doilies on the chairs. Funny, though, to see all them big-bellied girls a-setting there knitting booties. I never did figger what happened to all them foundlings. Girls took most of 'em, I guess. One or two, I suspicion, are being raised here in White Sulphur.

Anyway, old Hook, he goes out there all the time and I never knew why, unless Maud Wall is full of unbridled carnal impulses. She's as tall as Hook, but not skinny, and with a bust that would make a younger man quiver.

For that matter, I never figured out Hook, either. Keeps to himself. Talks good, like he's got some education somewheres. Back east, I think. The way he stands, now there's a clue — I figgered he was an officer in the war, Union of course. The way he sets a horse and the way he stares down people. . . .

Any rate, Hook never goes the other direction, for a bath and a barbering and a visit to Molly's and her girls — like the rest of us, when we want to make a good evening of it. No, Hook goes to see Maud, and what the hell he does there with her and those bulging girls, I can't imagine. Stays the night, too. At least I seen that ugly roan of his in the pen many a time when I'm on the prowl, checking on them women. I sort of enjoy doing that. Checking up there, I mean.

Well, Hook had disappeared up the street. It was still pouring so you couldn't see the mountains, and I went back to my solitaire.

That business down on the Smith River, there was only one way it could go. They'd break Hook. They never did cotton much to him, especially with him having those two Blackfeet Injuns for help. Not real white drovers, but two Injuns, and Blackfeet at that, as if nothing ever happened with them Piegans and no one remembers nothing. But there was old Hook down there, alone in that massive log ranch house, and them copper-colored bucks in a little bunk shack over to the barn. Them bucks were so poor at cow handling that some of the Texas hands around and about took pity on 'em, and showed 'em how. Funny, the Texas hands all herding Herefords now, and the Injuns herding the old Texas longhorns. Must be nearly the last bunch of longhorns in Montana, except maybe on the reservations.

Deputizing Hook. Now that was something. Maybe it'd bring it to a boil. Been simmering long enough. It was Bark that done it. Hamilton Bark. Been threatening to shoot them big bony critters for months, and maybe shoot Hook, too. Oh, maybe some others done it. Maybe Lorenzo Strunck or Dale Kratz. If it got down to the nasties, it'd be one of them I figgered. Twenty, thirty tough men − counting hands − against an old fool and two Injuns who didn't know diddly-spit.

No sooner did I get seven piles of cards dealt out again when there was a ruckus outside, where it was still pouring. The door flew wide and Ham Bark stomped in swearing blue streaks, followed by Hook, quiet as a mouse, with that mean scattergun pointing at Ham's kidneys. I filled my hand with my six-gun, just

14

in case there were jokers here. Bark was two hundred pounds of mean, in his thirties, bald as a pumpkin, and about as orange as one.

"Dammit, Oglesby, what is this?" he roared, not quite shattering glass.

Hook never said nothing, just prodded the big rancher toward the cells at the back, at least until Bark stopped cold at my desk.

"Found him in Jethro's," said Hook.

"Jethro's?" I asked, amazed.

"Yeah, Jethro's," snarled Bark, "embalming the bulls he says I shot. You deputize him?"

I grinned. "Deputized himself, mostly."

"If you move sudden, Bark, so will my trigger finger," Hook said. He continued to me, "I've arrested him. Charge him with ten bulls."

"What the hell!" Bark roared. "I'll get you, Oglesby."

"Not my doing," I said. Then I turned toward Hook. "What's your evidence? I can't charge a man, can't even hold him on suspicion, if there's no evidence."

Bark's face had gone from orange back to pink by then. "Act your age, Hook," he growled.

"He was having his dog embalmed. That's my evidence," said Hook.

"Dog? Embalmed? At Jethro's?" I sputtered.

"My Blackfeet man shot the dog whilst Bark

15

was shooting the bull."

"What the hell —"

"Bark likes that dog," Hook replied. "Was having him embalmed and having a dog-box built for burying."

Ham Bark's face turned orange again.

"He was loading the box in his spring wagon when I arrested him." Hook prodded Bark toward a cell.

"Whoa up," I snapped. "That's not evidence, Hook. You gone crazy or something?"

Hook stared me down again, which made me testy. I lifted my six-gun to stop that crazy old man.

"Don't," he said, his finger tightening.

"Don't!" cried Bark.

"How come you didn't report that your man shot the dog of whoever was shooting your bull?" I asked.

"You didn't ask." He prodded big Bark into a cell, and I let it happen.

"Key," he demanded. I tossed it, and he locked up Bark. "Write up a complaint," he said. "Ten bulls."

Bark was smart enough to keep his yap shut. But he was steamed up. Well, hell, he'll cool down, I thought. First, I had to get Hook out of there.

"Okay, Hook, you've got your man. Turn in

16

your star and the paper now that it's all over."

"Not yet," muttered the old boy. "Bark wasn't the only one. I've got a mess of others to arrest still."

Now that was news I didn't like; all them voters down there.

"You won't last long," snarled Bark, rattling the iron door. "You're a loner, and loners don't last."

"Hereford bulls die as easy as longhorns do," Hook replied. "Be grateful. Your Hereford bulls are alive, and your doggie is in heaven."

Now that was strange jabber if ever I've heard it. The old man was loco, I figgered.

"Sausage dogs. What's the name of those German sausage dogs?" Hook asked.

"Dachshunds," I said.

"Yes, well, Herefords are to cattle what dachshunds are to dogs. Bark here raises tall dogs, like out in the box there, and short beeves."

That was about the longest speech I'd ever heard Hook make, and maybe the most profound.

Hook spiked me again with his hazel eyes, and his mustache prickled out. "Leave him in there ten minutes. I'm going home. Let him out sooner and there'll be blood on your streets and Jethro will have more work."

17

"I'll kill you, Hook," snarled Bark.

"Longhorns taste better," the old man replied. He buttoned up his yellow slicker and slid quietly out into the drizzle.

"Lemme outa here, Will."

I sighed. "Maybe he has a point about ten minutes, Ham. I don't want no blood. . . . You shoot them bulls of his?"

"Not saying."

"Well, don't do it no more. Squeeze him some other way."

"He's holding up progress. Lemme out."

"Relax. I ain't writing any of this up, Ham. None of this never happened. Remember that when you vote."

"He killed Prince. I'll get him for that."

"I don't rightly remember him saying he killed that dog, Ham."

"His Injun did. Same difference. I'll kill all three of them."

"That'd please Jethro," I joked as I unlocked. "Now you go bury Prince, and leave old Hook alone."

Hamilton Bark grinned as he swept out the door.

CHAPTER 2

I hated like hell to go, but I didn't have no choice, not if I wanted to hang on to my star.

"Them Smith River ranchers are having a little powwow at Hamilton Bark's," I told Jasper Jethro, "and they've sent me a polite invite."

Jasper always took over for me as a temporary under-sheriff when I was out of town. There was never any trouble, neither. Like as if people figgered he was looking for funeral business while he patrolled the neighborhood. Jasper did nothing to discourage the idea, neither, although I personally know he made most of his money selling laudanum cut down with alcohol to the ladies.

"They're going to kill old Hook some day," he said. "Hook's without issue."

"What's that got to do with it?" I asked.

"Lots of things."

"Well, I'll be back in a day or two."

I headed for the livery where old Tin Flynn had my rig ready. Tin was born Tim, but the M got lost.

She was the nicest little carriage you ever did see, with oversized wheels and a padded leather seat on light leafsprings. But best of all was the little pivot-up hood with isinglass windows so I could get out snug as a bug in Montana weather. I always had spare gear in there, too. That was the way to travel. Better than forking a miserable horse for twenty-five miles. My big bay was all harnessed up nice in the traces.

"Thanks, Tin," I said. "I'm going out to settle down them hotheads on the Smith. Might even bring one of 'em back in cuffs," I added confidentially.

"Yeah? That's real interesting. You can tame 'em, Will."

I snapped the reins and the bay lurched out at a bright jog, and I pointed him south. Old Tin, he liked it when I hinted at what I was up to, and by the time it got told around town, it was always ten times bigger than it started. That's how to stay in office, I figgered. Get along with people. Line 'em up on your side.

What a great Montana spring day it was, with the air cool and dry and the sun blistering in, the big sky bluer than blue, and moldering old snowbanks retreating in the hollows. The gumbo was still soft, but them oversized wheels took it all easy. I had the pivoting hood down so's the sun could warm my old red neck and I could see the brown prairie – great tilted slabs of it, not a bit flat – and see the hawks rolling easy in the thick blue. The Smith River, which I followed, wasn't much of a stream in any case, but now it was roiling and tan with runoff. Off to the west, like a blue streak, was the Big Belts – a dreary bunch of mountains, like the Little Belts. But a few miles out I began to raise the Crazies far to the south in Yellowstone country. Now them were mountains as nice as God ever planted. Real, honest, snowcapped peaks, good for gazing at.

Down there in the Smith River grazing district I could see all them white-face Herefords dotting the tawny prairies that were starting to green up some. And sometimes in their midst were them longhorns of Hook's, steers and cows mostly, big and rangy, with them horns they didn't hesitate to gouge into them shorthorns – which was another sore point riling up the ranchers down there. Everybody was damn mad.

I checked to make sure my scattergun was under the seat. It was. I had the six-gun and holster on the plush leather beside me: hate the weight of it banging on my hip. Only time now I ever wear it is patrolling the town, and I do that less and less now they got a constable. Shotguns are better anyway for sheriff work. I never did see a man but respected one pointing his way.

Down a mile, where Smith River crooks east and begins to fizz out in those hills, was Hamilton Bark's spread. Nice place. Kept up nice and progressive. Ham's a man looking to the future. Maybe that's why he heads up the Smith River grazing district. Actually, it could just as well be called the Shields River district, that's how far south it goes. Ham's clapboard place with whitewashed outbuildings was in the middle of the district. Hook, he was down there at the headwaters of Sixteen Mile Creek, south of Horse Butte in an old log house, with everything same as when he settled in the early seventies.

They were all there. I could see that as I wheeled in. Pen full of horses and one buggy — Widow Thwait's I figgered. She was a mean woman, the worst of the soreheads. One thing did surprise me, though: Hook's ugly roan gelding was tied up there. My stomach knotted up some. It'd been a dandy spring day so far, and now it'd be like a late blizzard in there. I buckled on the six-gun again, thinking it added a little weight to my voice there. A little lead ballast never hurt a sheriff none.

Sure enough, Hook was inside, sitting off in a kind of unspoken isolation. His rheumy old eyes were taking it all in, even though no one was bothering to speak with him. Come to his own lynching, I thought. Ham patted me on the back and thrust some corn spirits in a cut-glass beaker at me. After we'd howdied for a while, they told me that fifteen out of nineteen Association members had come.

We were all crowded into Mrs. Bark's parlor, sitting on the rosewood furniture, those who had seats. The smoke was thick and smarty so I opened a sash window some, figgering Widow Thwait would prefer it. She favored me with a smile, which was a rarity, considering what that old horse was like, and I smiled back, thinking she had a nice spread and two grown sons and an empty four-poster I seen once.

"Let's get going," Ham said, getting us quiet. "Will, we got you down here to get the drift of things. And give us some satisfaction."

"Hope I can, Ham," I said genially. "That's what you elected me for."

It occurred to me that maybe I should sort of run this show, seeing as how I was guest of honor. They were a tough bunch, sitting there in the middle of the blue smoke. I knew pretty well who the powers were; the rest were the followers and fence-sitters I didn't care about, except as voters. Ham was one of the leaders. Bert Stern and Dan Monk, who ran the big Monk and Stern spread, were two more. And Widow — Mary Ellen, actually — Thwait. She was a firebrand, and I suspicioned she might be a bit demented. Abe Stapp, who had a spread close to town, would side with them as would Stope and Jung from the Sixteen Mile Creek country.

"What about deputizing Hook? How come you did that?" It was black-haired, bulbous-nosed Stern speaking. Captain Stern, late of the Union Army dragoons. "What right's he got to go around arresting us on some fool charge or other?"

I was ready for that. "No right," I replied. "Hell, fellas, he just barged in and pinned his star on. I was just humoring him. Right, Sam?"

The old boy just glared.

"Well, Sam, I'll take that star now." I held out my hand.

He didn't move, and I didn't want to make it look like a tug of wills, so I just sort of blandly stepped over there and lifted that star off his vest in a sociable way. The old man watched me quietly, and I decided that age maybe gave him some sense after all.

"That satisfy you all?" I asked cheerily.

It seemed to. Nobody said nothing. I figgered as long as I was holding the floor, I'd put in my two cents for law and order.

"Now the reason he got deputized," I continued, "is that ten of his bulls got shot and this country here is a far piece from White Sulphur. Now I don't like bulls being shot, property being destroyed and all that in my county, so I'm posting a twenty-five dollar reward for information leading to the conviction of them that done it." I fixed an eye on Hook. "That sound about right, Sam?"

I guess it wasn't, judging from that baleful look he gave me.

"Ten bony longhorns ain't worth twenty-five dollars," snapped Widow Thwait. "What're you backin' him for?"

"Ain't backing' anybody," I retorted. "Law's neutral. Two-way street, too. If any other bulls, like them Herefords of yours, gets shot, I'll be knocking on someone's door fast enough."

With that I sat down on the piano stool feeling pretty good. The reward, it wasn't enough to bother them none or cost me votes, but it went on record that I was seeing to justice and being a good peace officer, fair to all comers.

I was expecting Bark to take over, but no, it was old Hook who creaked upright and seemed to stare at the wall, no one in particular, until everyone was transfixed by his presence. Like I said, he could fill a room, and it was something to watch, the way those he-lions there sat stony-faced and studying the roses in the carpet.

Then, in that reedy, cracked voice of his, he gave them the shortest what-for I'd ever heard.

"Public land," the old man began. "I have a perfect right to run longhorns there. No law covers it. If you want purebreds, fence your patent land and breed inside your wire. Shooting my bulls is a criminal offense and an unneighborly act."

He paused, looking them over one by one.

"Longhorns survive these winters. If progress is wet-nursing Herefords, then I'm against that kind of progress. . . . Kill any more of my bulls, and lightning will strike you."

He stood there staring at them, but they were all studying the roses.

"Good day, gents," he said softly and glided out, light and stiff. A moment later we heard the quiet clop of hooves on the clay road.

Now that, I thought, was a record-breaker short speech. The man'd never be a good politician. Made his case, too, I figgered. And a little threat to go with it, whatever he meant by lightning striking. I reckon now if lightning struck anyone dead, I'd be out at Hook's with a murder warrant. I had to respect the old coot, mesmerizing them all with that reedy voice and those two watery arc lights of eyes.

Hamilton broke the spell. "Well," he said, "now the old boy's gone we can get down to business. Sheriff, we none of us take kindly to those remarks of yours. That's why we brought you out here.

"This thing's been going two years now, and those scrub bulls of his are costing us thousands of dollars. Not just us, either. The whole county. The White Sulphur merchants, the bank. . . .

"We've been patient; we've tried to talk that stubborn old man into some sense, some idea of progress and modern breeding and genetics and integrated herds and all the rest. And he just snorts.

"We tried to get a law passed in Congress allowing grazing districts to set their own standards. No dice.

"And now we've had it. We can't have one man holding up the whole county just because he is standing on some sort of mythical rights he thinks he has. We're taking steps. And you're going to choose up sides if you want to be sheriff next term. We're telling you here and now to stay out of this country until we do what we have to do. It's going to be none of your business. Some rules may be bent a little until that old goat bends or breaks. And you'll either be with us, or against us. Which'll it be?"

Well, old Ham had me there. I sat there on the whirly piano stool looking at the biggest bunch of staring eyes and thundercloud frowns I ever did see. Between them, and their ranch hands, and the merchants in town, and the bankers, they owned the votes.

"My oath of office says I got to uphold the law," I said, my mind made up, "and I can't be allowing no rule-bending, least any I'm aware of. I'll stay up in White Sulphur."

That was my answer, and a dandy, too.

"You'll not come down here," said Bert Stern flatly. "And up there, you're going to be our eyes and ears."

"Well," I said, "if you think you can handle it proper, you won't be needing no law. You're all salt of the earth and will do things good and decent, and that's good enough for me. Now, I can't make no promises about not coming here, in my jurisdiction – you know that – but if you give me no reason to poke around, I ain't coming."

Widow Thwait and Ham Bark glanced at each other.

"Sorry, Will," she said. "That's not enough."

"What's not – ?"

"Keeping your nose out isn't enough. We elected you and we'll unelect you. Ham

28

will run against you."

"Well, now —" This was the beginning of a pickle that was getting hard to suck. "This star is nothing I need that bad, Mary Ellen," I intoned. "Got lots of irons in the fire."

"Running irons must likely," she retorted. "That old duffer has got to be stopped. Clay Cott, over to the bank, says he can make stock loans half a percent lower on purebred herds. Every scrub crossbreed we end up with costs us ten or fifteen dollars. Are you understanding me?"

"Absolutely, Widow."

"Good. You're going to help get this over with. You're going to start tracking down Sam Hook. No one knows a thing about him. For all we know, he could be a face on an old flyer. Cott says that Hook pays sixty dollars a month to Maud Wall, regular as the moon cycle. You find out why. You find out where he's from and what he's hiding.

"And that's not all. You swear out warrants against those Blackfeet bucks. For shooting longhorn bulls. For shooting Ham's dog. They both got Winchester seventy-three carbines, forty-four forties, so they's likely guilty. And if Maud Wall don't talk, you swear out charges against her, too. Running a bawdy house and public nuisance. And you find out exactly what

Hook's got patented and if he owes taxes and if he's fenced any public land. You do that and maybe you can stay sheriff. Meanwhile, we got our own fish to fry with the railroad, the brand inspectors, and the feed store."

My palms were sweating a little, but I didn't want them to know it.

"I'll see that justice is done, Widow Thwait," I said, forcing a smile.

The contempt on her face was a thing to behold, and I knew in a flash I'd stepped on a cowpie.

"Justice hell," she spat. "Progress is what we're after, and don't you forget it."

"It's getting late, Will," said Ham, "And you've got a long buggy ride on up to White Sulphur. Nice you could come on down. The rest of us, we're going to stay on here and talk livestock, and that'd just bore you, I'm sure. I'll be up there, two or three days, to see how you're doing."

Just like that.

"Well, it's all for a good cause," I said. No one smiled. In fact, no one said nothing, and that riled me some. Almost like they were disrespectful of the star. They should be more grateful for peace and law and order, I thought.

"Be seeing ya, Sheriff," Ham finally said.

"Glad to pitch in and help out."

Outside, the hostler saw me coming and by the time I got there he had the big bay backed into the traces.

"Nice rig there, Mr. Sheriff."

"Takes me anywhere the law's needed, boy," I said. "I bought it with my own funds. My contribution to the county."

With that I was off into the fresh afternoon.

CHAPTER 3

Maud Wall served me India tea, genteel-like in a cup and saucer.

"Spode," she said.

"Spode what?"

"Spode china. Now then, Sheriff, what may I do for you?"

"Well, I just thought I'd pay a little visit."

"That's unusual."

"Oh, I've been meaning to, long time. How's business, Maud?"

"I wouldn't call what I do a business, Sheriff Oglesby. A living, yes."

There she was, being contrary already. I just knew taking her and them girls in wasn't going to be easy, even if they were only women.

"How many you got now?"

"Two," she replied. "Caroline and Constance. We use first names only. You understand."

" 'Deed I do," I said, slurping a little. The girls were nowhere in sight. I wanted a little look-see. Always interesting what kind of women do it and get caught. Well, I'd see them soon enough, I figgered.

"I don't think you're here to pass the time of day," she said. She was the first amber-eyed person I'd ever met, and them yellow eyes were on me like a pair of hot gun muzzles. I stared around the parlor a little. Big overstuffed horsechair sofa and chairs like a man would choose. Lace curtains, and a bunch of lilacs in a vase.

"Election year, Maud," I said.

She smiled.

"Say, I seen Sam Hook's roan out in your pen a lot," I said.

"You've come to find out things about Mr. Hook."

"Naw, wouldn't say that."

"You are interested in our relationship."

"I seen that horse. He spends a lot of time here."

She smiled. "And from that you have inferred things."

"No, ma'am. Old Sam, he's riling up some people and I'm just keeping the peace, is all."

She fixed those amber eyes on me until I could hardly stand it.

"Keeping the peace. That's what you're do-ing," she said, amusement lifting the edges of her lips.

There she was, making fun of me, and that

33

made me mad, damn that amber-eyed cat.

"Well," I said, "just what's he do around here? Why's he paying you sixty dollars a month?"

She recoiled, just barely, but I saw it.

"Who told you that?"

"Just something I know."

"You got it from the bank," she said, toying with a gold pocket watch she wore as a pendant on her bosom. "I will change banks."

"I was just wondering —"

"Whether I'm a bought woman." She stared out the window for a bit, a window that opened out upon the Little Belts to the north.

"I will tell you about this . . . business, as you call it. When a girl comes here, I charge her twenty-five dollars a month for her keep and deliver her when her time comes. I shouldn't say girls. Women. Women with no place to go. Women whose lives suddenly collapsed; who were thrown out of homes, beaten, abused. Women whose families have arranged a lengthy vacation. Usually there are four or five here.

"Some can pay. They've got a little stowed away. Or the man — the . . . paramour — helps out. The cowboys pay. Sometimes a father pays. Sometimes a mother slips her daughter a little. And that's what I live on.

"But some girls can't pay and I can't afford to take them in. They're homeless, out in the streets, starving and desperate. It's either die out there, or a deal with Molly and her kind — a spare room for a while and then a degraded life. Those ones, the desperate ones, are Sam's charities. For the sixty a month he provides, I take any young lady in need."

She sat quietly, letting all that settle in. I didn't know whether to believe her or not. No man in his right mind spends good money on keeping harlots respectable.

"Funny business," I said.

"Not funny if a man has had his way with you and you're pregnant and it's showing and you are thrown out of your home and must hide from your neighbors," she said firmly.

"Seems to me once they're fallen, they should stay fallen. I can't rightly see them hiding out and getting all respectable again, fooling some decent man."

"That's their business, not yours."

There she was, being contrary again. That Maud Wall was no female I'd ever have around.

"The young ladies are not idle here," she continued. "They garden in the summer, put up preserves, gather eggs, chop firewood and empty ashes, bake and cook, all as part of their keep. I teach them the three Rs and social graces. And of course they sew for themselves and their babies. When they leave, they are better off than before."

She said it so matter-of-factly you'd never think them doxies ever whooped it up with a man. But to me, once a harlot, always a harlot.

"You disapprove," she said.

I frowned. "It don't make sense, Hook paying good money for that. Why's he really doing it?"

"Must you have a reason?"

The way she said it, all icy and smart, just riled me all the worse until I was fixing to put cuffs on her before I was ready.

"He's not competent, Hook," I said. "Senile. We're fixing to have him put away or have a guardian appointed."

"We? Being whom?"

"Well, everybody. Them ranchers he's hurting."

"And you."

"Well, I'm just getting to the bottom of things for them, on behalf of everybody, county welfare and all."

"He is perfectly competent," she said. It wasn't an opinion, neither. She was just saying it like a fact of life. "More tea?"

I declined.

"You are fishing for information you

hope will damage him."

That woman sure had a tongue in her.

"The law has taken sides," she added.

"Now doggone it, Maud, I enforce the law without fear or favor, impartial as can be."

She rose. "Well then, good day, Sheriff. It was nice of you to visit."

"Now just wait a minute, Maud; I'm not done yet, not by a long shot."

She settled back on the edge of her chair, cat-watching me.

"Now Hook ain't got any relatives; no issue as far as anyone knows. Old man all alone down there. He fixing to give you his place when he goes?"

"That's not your business."

"Yes, it is. I seen the will and he's fixing to favor you and this harlot house. The county can't have no bequests to —"

She paled. "You do have ways of getting information. Who told you?"

"I ain't saying."

"Mr. Hook has one copy. His attorney has another. I will let Mr. Hook know. He will change lawyers."

I grinned. "Didn't mean to upset you, Maud. Just doing my job is all. Lots of people pretty unhappy with that old man. His scrub bulls all over the range are costing all them ranchers thirty, maybe forty thousand a year, and that hurts the merchants and the tradespeople, and the taxes too, so I'm getting hurt. He's holding up —"

"Progress. But he's violating no law."

"Well, we'll see about that. Could be he's senile and needs a guardian."

"I see," she said, studying me close. "Well, good day, Sheriff Oglesby."

"I ain't done yet."

"I believe a man's home is his castle. And a woman's too. Or is a woman's home subject to different common law rights, Sheriff?"

She sure was an educated one, knowing all that stuff. She talked city, like an easterner. I ignored her.

"You will leave my home at once," she said.

"This ain't a home," I replied. "Now produce them girls. I want to see them. I want their full names and addresses too. Could be runaways or vagrants. People without means, that's against the law. Runaway wives, we get ahold of the husband so he can fetch her back."

"No."

"You resisting? Then I'll be doing it myself."

She reconsidered. "Wait," she said, and slipped away up them stairs, her skirts rustling. A few minutes later she herded the two women into the parlor. One chubby one was about seven months along, I figgered. The one in the dove-gray dress. The other, in dark green, she hardly showed, and she was a looker too, chestnut hair flowing down in ringlets and a nice face with wide eyes. But now she was looking scared and the other was bawling.

"This is Constance Jones and Caroline Smith," Maud said tautly.

"Names you give 'em don't make no difference. I'll get your records and find out the real ones. Now I got you together I'm taking you in on charges. Running a disorderly house and whatever else."

It was if lightning had hit Maud, and for once them cat-eyes looked wild.

"Complaints? Who?" she asked bitterly.

"Ain't rightly saying. Good citizens and upright. Voters been complaining about this here scandalous place."

"You have warrants I presume?"

"Right here, Maud." I pulled them out of my breast pocket. "Signed by Jefferson Bark. Judge Bark."

"Hamilton's brother," she said bitterly. "You've closed down Molly's place I presume?"

"Well no, not rightly. No complaints about her as I know of."

"I see." Her face was something not to stare at, I'll tell you. I got to thinking that if she had a lady gun she'd have shot me. But her and them sniffling girls, they just stood there.

"Put out your hands, Maud. I'm putting cuffs on you. I don't rightly trust you'll behave."

She did, full of huff and fury, and I snapped the iron shut, feeling better.

"Now I'll just be fetching your records and whatever evidence I can find."

That was easy. In a leatherbound ledger, in an awkward hand — funny, she was a midwife but wrote awkward — were names, dates, amounts paid, and by who. All there. And deposit receipts showing Hook's sixty dollars going in. Wages of sin, I figgered.

She addressed the girls: "We've done nothing wrong. We shall walk with our heads up and we will be composed. People will stare, and they will note your delicate condition, and they will be thinking things. Ignore them. And trust in ultimate justice."

The snuffling one, Constance, she stopped and mopped her eyes.

"Let's go, ladies," I said cheerily.

"You are a venal man, Sheriff."

"What's venal mean?"

She smiled bitterly. "It means you are a . . . whore."

"Now you just shut your yap or I'll add

to the charges," I snarled.

It was a good time to be marching them in. Midafternoon, and White Sulphur full of good folk who watched my little parade march by. The youngsters, they whistled. The men standing on the boardwalks, they grinned. But the women watched silently. Good thing they couldn't vote. Them girls, they didn't exactly look scarlet but those bellies told the tale well enough. I'll give 'em credit, though. Like Maud, the two girls were walking head up, eyes front, proud hussies all three.

I booked them in and patted them down for concealed stickers, that sort of thing, which was sort of entertaining. Then I put Maud in cell number one and the two girls in number two. That left number three for drunks and emergencies. There wasn't no privacy, but I figgered women of that sort didn't need it. That one wench, Constance, she was sobbing again, but I didn't pay no mind.

"We have a right to a speedy arraignment and a right to post bail," Maud said.

I don't know where she knew all that stuff. I ignored her. I figgered to let her set there a day or two, just to knock her down a few pegs.

"And counsel," she said. "I wish to speak with Francis Harp as soon as possible."

Harp? I thought. That old drunk? Why'd she

41

pick him? So plastered he'd lost his practice and could scarcely stand upright in court.

"I'll get to it when I get to it," I replied. I meant to let that she-cat stew.

"Francis Harp is a drunk," she said quietly, amber eyes glowing again. "And the reason he's a drunk is that he can't be bought or sold in a county that buys and sells law. I will trust him. I wish Mr. Hook had retained him."

I just grinned. By her lady logic, it made sense. But that wasn't the way to get along. Get a lawyer with connections, with influence. Harp, he had less influence than a carpet beetle.

I stepped out into the spring sunshine and locked the jailhouse door behind me. Didn't want no gawkers going in there to stare at the women. It was a rare day with the big sky stretching off to tomorrow, and them foothills dotted with ponderosa rising up, blue layers, inviting a man to ride high, free as a meadowlark. That's what Montana is all about, progress and freedom and law and order.

I ambled on down to Jethro's, six-gun banging on my hip, glaring at people who rushed up with a question on their lips. Part of being sheriff was being mysterious and strong.

Jethro sidled up at once. He was a skinny critter with oiled down black hair and a lot of black fuzz around his nostrils.

"The women, what's that all about?"

"Tell you later. I'm going on down to Hook's place for a day or two, maybe faster. I want you should feed them and take care of the place."

"Feed the women?"

"Yeah, on the county prisoner account. And look to their needs. I don't want them getting sick or nothing in their condition. Voters wouldn't like it."

"You're off to Hook's? What's he got to do with it?"

"Tell you later," I said. "It's juicy, his lash-up with Maud. He'll likely cave in on his herd bulls, he hears about the women. And if he don't, I got a couple more surprises for him in my vest-pocket."

"They been arraigned or anything?"

"Naw, and don't do it. Just hold 'em. Hook'll cave in and I'll just let the women off with vagrancy or something like that."

"Hostages, like?"

"Hostages ain't a bad word for it, but don't say it. Not exactly proper in some people's way of thinking."

"Okay," Jethro said. "I'll feed them well and keep them fit. What's the charges in case anyone asks?"

"Oh, Maud: keeping a disorderly house, re-

43

sisting arrest. The other two: vagrancy, lewd conduct, disturbing the peace."

"Is that so?" Jethro was amazed.

"Oh, and one more thing, Jasper. Maud wants to see that old fogey Francis Harp. Go get the old soak and let her talk to him. It won't do no harm, and then it's on the record she got counsel."

"Sure enough, Will. I'll dry him out and plop him in her boudoir." He chuckled lecherously. "I always thought there were pretty fancy goings-on at Maud's. Stuff that would make Molly's look like an ice cream social."

CHAPTER 4

I had never been to Hook's ranch, and I found it admiresome. The house was square and built of massive logs, the sort that only a team rigged to a block and tackle could have lifted into place. And they had been carefully adzed, top and bottom, so that they pressed together and required little chinking.

Along the front was a roofed porch. The windows were shuttered with heavy plank, and there were loopholes visible. The massive pole corrals and log barn were equally sturdy. Hook had built the place to last forever. There was a nice lookout, too, on down to Sixteen Mile Creek and off to the wooded foothills beyond.

He had seen me coming and was waiting on his porch, which surprised me some. I fastened my six-gun belt back on before stepping from the buggy, just in case. Hook motioned to a Blackfeet buck who appeared out of nowhere, and the Injun unbuckled my bay from the traces and led it to the pen, which was some bothersome to me. He was no boy, neither, and that also surprised me. He was a gray-haired old buck, maybe sixty. He wore his hair in two braids with a black bowler perched above, and a red calico shirtwaist belted in, and jeans. Expressionless, too, flat black eyes telling me nothing.

"What can I do for you, Oglesby?" Hook asked in that old, cracked voice, squinting up at me. He looked kind of frail in the flesh, but strong somehow with that massive house behind him.

"Hello Sam," I said.

"I'm not Sam to you now," he responded. "From now on it's Mr. Hook."

"Aw, Sam, I'm just visiting."

"It's Mr. Hook. And you're not visiting. Your purpose is not social. Come in."

It was pretty dark in there with all them logs walling out the sun and the sky. But there was a wide fieldstone fireplace with a long lazy fire in it taking off the spring chill.

"Nice outfit here —," I said. I was going to call him Sam and swallowed up on it.

"State your business, Oglesby." Them hazel eyes and the reedy voice had an edge to them, I'd say.

I took a seat on the quilted cowhide sofa, even if I wasn't invited. Figgered some palaver would thaw the ice. He stood.

46

"This place is really solid," I commented. "Log house like this stands handsome against the cold. Sort of old-fashioned, though, not like them carpenter gothic places modern folk are building in town."

The corners of his eyes crinkled.

"This place has character," I added.

"Character, yes. That's a word for it. What's your business, Oglesby?"

"Sheriff Oglesby, dammit," I snapped.

"When you're here on sheriff business, I'll use the title." He said it so softlike it took me a moment to figger what he didn't say. "I imagine your new masters have sent you here to find out about me."

"Naw, just a social visit —"

"Either you're here to impart information or obtain it."

"Well, you put it that way, if you want. I'm lining up facts so's to keep the peace. Things are getting to boiling around here ..."

"You said that before. What Bark probably wants you to find out is anything he can throw at me: my land patents, taxes, my past, my family. That about right?"

"Well —"

His eyes glinted in dark amusement.

"I'm not secret," he said, meditatively. "Sit still there for two minutes and you'll learn all

47

there is to know about me."

I grinned amiably.

"Born eighteen and twenty, upstate New York, town of Friendship. Son of a harness-maker and smith and firewood dealer. I fled to St. Louis at sixteen and hired on as a camptender with a Rocky Mountain fur brigade. I caught the last three, four rendezvous as a trapper. By eighteen and forty the beaver trade had faded, but I continued, through my twenties, to scratch a living at it. . . ."

A mountain man, I thought. That explained some.

"Married four years. Mrs. Hook died in childbirth, eighteen and forty-eight, four decades ago. I never remarried."

That jolted me.

"I stayed in the territory and ranched. When the Texas herds arrived in the seventies I bought longhorns and built here. Finest country in Montana Territory.

"I'm self-educated. See those books?"

I hadn't, but now I was staring at a whole wall of them.

"I know a little about a lot of things, but not a whole lot about a single subject, the way college graduates do.

"Character, yes. A good word for what I strive toward. Character. The longhorns have character. Slow to grow, tall of frame, big boned, with less meat. But they survive and prosper and fatten here without any hand-holding. They're the future, not those sausage cows from the British Isles."

He stared at me intently, obviously making his case. For the record, mainly, since it wouldn't do no good.

"The Blackfeet who took your horse. His name is Padlock. He's my brother-in-law."

"What!"

"He is my wife's brother. She was a Piegan."

My jaw must have been hanging loose, it surprised me so much. I shifted my weight and swung my holster around so it didn't dig into my thigh.

"I was married by Father de Smet, the missionary to the Blackfeet and Flatheads," he added gently, reading my mind.

I was a little disappointed to hear that.

"Padlock's son Jerome works for me as well. My nephew by marriage. Both are able men." The crowsfeet crinkled around his eyes.

"They and Maud Wall each get a third of this when I go."

Another jolt the old man threw at me. But that one tickled me. That will was gonna get busted. Who'd defend a couple of bucks and a sharp-tongued old harlot?

"All three are strong and capable. They'll hang on, even after the will-breakers who own you do their dirty work."

I bridled at that. "Now see here, Sam. I'm my own man."

He stared. "That roan of mine that you hate —"

"Who says I hate your roan?"

"You hate him. He's not pretty. Hammerhead. All sinew. Long of flank and rawboned. All he has is character. He goes and goes, gives his all, and when the going is tough, he tries all the harder. An improvement over carpenter gothic."

"You're crazy, Sam, willing this place to two Injun bucks and that woman."

"Crazy? Go ahead and think it. It saves me explaining myself. Now have you discovered what you came to worm out of me?"

"Wouldn't put it that way, Sam —"

"Sure, sure."

"You gonna give this place to them ignorant bucks?"

"Mr. Padlock has read this entire library. He does most of my accounting and correspondence. And Mrs. Wall —"

"Mrs? She married?"

"A widow. Her husband was a professor of

50

medicine at Johns Hopkins."

"At who?"

He smiled. "A university."

"She have influence and all that?"

"I don't know what you mean."

"Her people, could they pull strings and such?"

That hawk-look rose in his eyes, and I didn't like it.

"Why do you ask a question like that?"

Well, I had his attention. I'd taken his guff long enough and now it was my turn.

"Well, now, Sam," I began expansively, "some good upright folk, they've complained about her and that shameful house she runs. Pressing me to clean up this here county for good churchgoing folk."

Now he was frowning and I had him good.

"Yesterday I got to investigating and she was running a shameful place all right, and I saw the records where you were paying her to do it —"

"Bull," he said.

"Sixty a month, and Clay Cott says so too. I taken them all in, Maud and them two fallen women she's got there, and I'm holding them on suspicion in the jailhouse and I come out to tell you they're all locked up."

Hook, he didn't say nothing. Just stared.

51

"Well?" I asked. "What are you going to do?"

He just stood there, that frail old fellow, staring. Didn't seem so large now. Then he lifted them eyes from me and gazed into the fire.

"What charges?"

"Keeping a disorderly house. Lewd conduct. Resisting arrest. Disturbing the peace."

"They've been arraigned? Bail set?"

"Nope. I was just holding 'em until I had a little chat with you. They're comfortable. Jethro's looking after them and keeping out the peepers."

I thought I saw a flash of fury cross his face, and it tickled me some, the cock of the walk crawling.

"Of course these fine citizens wanted Molly's place shut down first," he mocked.

"Nope. No complaint there. She's an honest whore, not pretending to be respectable."

"I see," he said and lapsed into brooding.

I fidgeted some.

"Well, I figger maybe you own Maud's place, the way you pump cash into it. So I figger maybe you'd want to get them women out. I could maybe let them off light, like with lewd conduct or some such, if you'd agree to a few things."

"The answer is no."

"Well, maybe they'll rot in there then. No rush to have them arraigned. She's got Harp. Lot of good that'll do."

"I'll see you to the door, Oglesby."

"Oh, I ain't done, Sam. Them bucks. You mind fetching them in here? I'm taking them in on suspicion of shooting your bulls. Warrants right here." I patted my vest-pocket.

"My brother-in-law and nephew shooting our bulls," Hook mocked. He laughed in that reedy wheeze of his. "Let me see," he said.

I handed him the warrants. "There it is — you brought me a mess of forty-four forty slugs, and them bucks have forty-four forty carbines."

He was grinning. "Signed by Jefferson Bark, magistrate," he wheezed.

Then he pitched them into the fire.

"Hey!" I hollered. "That's legal paper. That's a criminal offense. That's a crime, Hook, and you're in for it now!"

He gazed at me calmly. "When you come to me as the sheriff of the commonwealth, I respect the office and the law. When you come to me as a fat errand boy, it's another matter."

"You get them bucks. I'm arresting you and them bucks, Hook. Right now."

I stood up — right into the gaping barrels of his sawed-off twelve gauge.

"Holding a weapon on me; resisting arrest —

you're in bad trouble, Hook. Put that down or it'll be worse."

He just stood there smiling, dementedlike. I always knew he was crazy.

"Drop the iron, Sheriff." He made a joke of my title.

I did. No sense messing with a loon like that. I unhooked the belt and let it slide down easy.

He circled around to the door, them black holes always pointing at me and making me sweat.

"Lock," he called softly. That Injun was inside in no time, kind of glidinglike.

"Get that iron, and his shotgun from the buggy, and any other toadstickers he has around. We're going to town. And saddle the roan, please."

He was back in a few minutes. My bay had been harnessed and Hook's roan saddled.

"We're going to release Maud and her girls," Hook announced. "No charges have been filed and none will be."

"You're under arrest, Hook. This is my last warning," I yelled. But he just blinked at me.

"I'll be riding right at your side and a little behind. Make one false move and you'll be dead. Drive directly to the jailhouse, not to Tin's."

He marched me off like a common prisoner

to the buggy, and I got in, slow and easy.

"One thing, Oglesby," he muttered from his saddle. "What did you hope to accomplish? The longhorn bulls for the women's freedom?"

I didn't answer him and he just grinned. But I figgered I'd get help in town, signal someone, and then that old boy would be in cell number three, fast as lightning. It'd be a long drive though and we'd get there around midnight, dang the luck.

It was long and cold. I thought some about just taking off, knowing that his scatter-gun had no range and I'd be safe in a few yards. But that roan of his, it'd keep up, and maybe he had a rifle sheathed on the far side of his saddle where I couldn't see. I wanted the hood up because it was nippy but I didn't dare, so mostly I sat there cussing the old loon and pointing the bay north until we clattered over the plank bridge to the east shore of the North Fork, and then up the long grade to town, all dark in the quarter-moon light.

Worst of all he sat there right behind me singing. That's right, just singing them cowboy tunes, like that one about Laredo. That voice of his, it was like chalk screeching across a blackboard.

It was almighty dark around the jailhouse. Jethro hadn't left no lantern burning or nothing. I got out thinking to bust around the corner before he could swing that gun around but he was watching and them two bores were blacker than the night.

"Unlock it, Oglesby."

"I don't have the key. Jethro's got it."

"Unlock it or you're dead."

I did. I walked into the blackness with him sticking that scatter-gun into my kidneys, and I found a lucifer, scratched it, and lit the lamp. Them women were all standing up and staring scaredlike.

"Unlock," Hook said again and I figgered to get over where he couldn't shoot without hitting the women too, but he suddenly waved me aside.

"Sit," he said, pointing to a visitor chair and I cursed the luck. I had a six-gun in my desk drawer, just begging to be got hold of.

"Drop the cell keys ten feet in front of you."

I did. He seemed testy and I didn't want to provoke him. This was getting embarrassing and I was already thinking about what to tell the voters. Not that anyone needed to know what was happening. Maybe I could just tell folks that the charges on the women had been dismissed, and I'd sent them home.

"Oh, Sam," Maud said aloud. "Oh, Sam."

"Here's the key, Maud. Reach through and

unlock yourself and the girls."

"No, Sam! This is jailbreaking! I've talked to Francis Harp and he's going to —"

"Do it," the old man rasped. "Oglesby's just using his sheriff star for the private purposes of some greedy people. Putting you in here had nothing to do with public justice."

"But what will happen, Sam? He'll just come get us again."

"No, he won't." He said to me, "You arrest these women again, or harass them or bother them, and your short fat life will come to an abrupt and painful end."

He meant it, too.

"Get in the cell. Jethro will let you out in the morning."

"What about my rig?"

"It'll be at Tin's and the horse cared for."

I stepped in and heard the long clang of iron in the gloom, and the click.

"I'll leave you a lantern," he said. "In case there are ghosts."

He shepherded the women out the door and into the night, and for a moment I could see stars glinting in the big sky, and the black foothills north of town rising endlessly across the wide land.

The jailhouse door banged shut and I heard them walking east to Maud's, and then silence.

Later I heard the rig being wheeled off to Tin's.

The old boy wasn't so smart, I figgered. A posse would get him in the morning. He was in trouble big enough to swallow him whole. I'd have to think some about what I'd say in the morning. It would be hard explaining them warrants charging them bucks with shooting bulls — how was I to know them bucks were related to him? I'd have to watch what I said, and watch how I told the story about ending up in this cell, too.

The damned bunk was solid plank, but I'd survive. Maybe I could turn this all around and get people to applauding what I done.

CHAPTER 5

Jasper Jethro chose that morning to be late. I was mad as hops, cold, and so starved I intended to chew an arm off Jethro if he didn't arrive with hot vittles and spring me from that damned cell.

When the door finally creaked open it wasn't Jethro; it was Francis Harp. And there I was, the sheriff of Meagher County, sitting behind bars, unshaven, and trying not to look sheepish.

"Harp. It's you, is it? Get me out of here," I roared.

He stopped to survey the situation — the women gone and me behind iron.

"This is quaint," he said.

"Quaint, hell. Lemme out of here. Key's lying on my desk."

He reflected a while as I stewed. Old Harp was a scarecrow with a Roman beak of a nose and clamshell pouches under his pale blue eyes. His dark hair was streaked with gray. There was nothing in his demeanor this morning to suggest he'd ever seen the inside of a bottle.

"I'll consider it," he said with a certain gleam in his eye. "It could be the county magistrates have arrested you for something or other, and if I were to unlock you, I'd be assisting in a jailbreak. I think I shall consult the magistrates before taking fateful steps."

"Unlock it," I howled. "It was an accident is all. A friendly joke." I'd decided not to tell anybody how come the women were free and I wasn't.

"My clients, I presume, are now at their residence?" he asked.

"How should I know? Lemme out!"

"I wouldn't think of it, Mr. Oglesby, without instructions."

"Well, get Jethro!"

"Alas, I saw him leave an hour ago driving that somber caisson of his — funeral business, I'm sure, Mr. Oglesby."

Damn the luck.

"Get me vittles! Get me Jefferson Bark! Charge it to the county!"

He considered the matter.

"I think it would be felicitous to conduct my business with you first, Mr. Oglesby," he said, settling into a visitor chair.

What made me mad was that there was a trace of a smile quivering on his lips. "Then

60

let's get it over with fast," I snapped.

"Tell me, are you a county prisoner?"

"Of course not!"

"How then did you come to this pass?"

"Ain't saying."

"Most extraordinary. An accident, you say?"

"Yeah, sure, accident."

"I see." He unfolded some gold-rimmed spectacles and withdrew a sheaf of papers from the vest-pocket of his threadbare suit.

"I represent two Jane Does and Maud Wall —"

"Dammit Harp, I'm arresting you for obstructing justice!"

"I see," he said. "Perhaps I'm obstructing injustice. Now then. Upon due consideration of the facts, I've elected an unorthodox defense of my clients to wit: I have in hand here a letter to the Territory attorney general, alleging malfeasance in office by Sheriff Oglesby, and citing unlawful detention, trumped up charges, and delayed arraignment of innocent parties. And further, to wit: a civil suit here, which I shall file in another venue, seeking damages of fifty thousand dollars for each of my clients for unlawful arrest and malfeasance by yourself and Magistrate Bark. And of course I shall conduct a traditional defense as well before his Holiness Jefferson Bark, if need be."

He paused. "And of course I've prepared copies of these documents which shall be handed to our beloved friend Max Perkins of the *Meagher County Tribune*."

I bridled at that, with all them voters reading it.

"Now then," he continued cheerfully, "would you mind telling me where you have spirited my clients?"

Now this was a pickle to suck on, I'll tell you.

"You wish to remain silent? It is your privilege. As it happens, my clients are at their home, their castle. Perhaps it'd be wise for you to tell me your version of last night's events."

Bluster seemed my only salvation. "You old lush," I roared, "you get Jeff Bark here now or I'll have you in trouble up to your ears. You fetch him now or you'll spend the rest of your life pounding rocks at Deer Lodge."

He smiled. "A sot I am, and a sot I will be again," he said. "It runs in the family. But, for the moment, I am engaged in a respite that will last until your ruin."

"Lemme out and I'll uncork a bottle and we'll just talk it over friendly," I said, grinning.

"Ah, the devil tempts," he replied. "That is a seductive proposition. But I shall abstain. Your wrath, I must say, is woefully misdirected. It is Mr. Jethro who has brought you to this low estate, for he has neglected his plain public duty and is pursuing his private interest. It is only by chance that my clients are not the pitiable creatures starving here, rather than yourself. Had he done his bounden duty, you would not suffer. So direct your wrath at the appropriate object, Mr. Oglesby. I am only a simple instrument of divine justice."

My stomach was hammering my backbone and I had a hunger headache so I elected to let the old creep ramble on. Maybe he'd get done and help me. Instead, he just sat there in the midday sun, quiet as could be, almost snoozing. I watched them dust motes whirl in the bright for a while and studied the Montana big blue out the window.

"The women are free and I ain't gonna file charges if you let me out of here," I said.

"I doubt you'd file charges in any case with Mr. Hook's threat hanging over you."

"You got the story then."

"Yes. Mrs. Wall hammered my door down at dawn and vividly, I must say, described the night's events. I shall add my own advice to Mr. Hook's. I shall refrain from filing these papers for as long as your conduct toward my clients is unblemished. Maxfield Perkins, great editor that he is, will publish the gravamen of the case against you if your conduct is not exemplary. A most civil thing to do, considering that he detests Mr. Hook."

Well, I thought, that wasn't too bad. No publicity yet.

"You win," I said. "Now, you going to let me out?"

"Shortly," he said. "First, I shall distribute these papers, and instructions, to parties unknown to you — just in case you contemplate violence upon my person. Then, I shall return and lecture you on the Golden Rule."

He bowed slightly and walked out, leaving me with a rumbling belly and a mess of worries, and them board planks to lie on. I needed to do some fast thinking but I was too mad to do any.

But it was Jethro who walked in next, interrupting a steak-and-potatoes fantasy.

"You idiot," I snapped. "Lemme out!"

He stared at me all agog, scurried like a black rat to the cell, and unlocked the door.

"Where've you been? How come you weren't here giving chow to the women this morning like I said?"

He crabbed away like a weasel as I stormed out and shoved him into a chair.

"Why . . . why, I had funeral business. The dead and the bereaved come first," he whined.

"Not before feeding county prisoners," I bellowed.

"But how was I to know — where are they?"

"Busted out, dammit."

"Well — I didn't — that Maud Wall needed to be taken down a peg. It'd serve her right, not getting —"

"You didn't follow my orders."

"I — I was just softening her up, eh? Softening her up for some —"

"I bet you were. Who died?"

"Why, uh, no one."

My bile boiled again.

"What do you mean, no one?"

"Why, bright and early, that hand of Widow Thwait's, Leonard Carroll, he rode in and told me Widow wanted a man-sized box. So I figured someone croaked. I took her a good golden oak one, befitting the prominent family and all, and I got Tin to rig up the black wagon and off I went. Now, who would have thought she just wanted the box and no one croaked? She laid out ten double eagles and Carroll and that other hand of hers, Kid Dunham, unloaded and carried it inside, and I drove back. Isn't that something? I mean, just buying a box? I bought it wholesale for thirty and shipping, so I made a bit out of the morning."

"Out. Get out."

"But . . . where's the women? How come you got locked in? Aren't you going to start a posse?"

"Out. I'll tell you later. And don't breathe a word of this, understand? You say one word and they'll be lowering you into your own box."

He skittered out. It was four in the afternoon and I was crazy-hungry so I buckled on my six-shooter and stomped over to Molly's. She'd serve a he-man meal even at four in the afternoon and not charge me, neither, because she respected the star.

She was just starting her day when I stalked into her saloon, which was covered by flocked fleur-de-lis wallpaper. The women were hardly up yet, but that's the way I wanted it. I was plumb out of sorts and didn't want company, least of all women. And short of shut-eye, too, with Hook's midnight ride and that bunch of planks to sleep on at the jail and all. Molly's Chinese cook brought me a plate of elk rump and potatoes, and I hitched my six-gun out of the way and dug in.

Molly, she just left me alone after eyeing me. She was smart. She didn't have much of a face with that weak chin and all but she had a splendid hourglass figure, even without the whalebone, and she dressed spiffy too. Today she was in bottle green velveteen with a scooped down neck to show off her freckled assets. Only woman I ever met with freckles just about everywhere, and a sultry foghorn voice, too. She was mostly out of the flatback side of it, except she saved some for Jeff Bark and me. I never figgered what she saw in that gimpy Jeff Bark, neither. But today I wasn't thinking much about Molly. Life had gotten heavy.

The fact of it was, I was sucking a sour pickle. I couldn't very well shush it up with Harp and Hook and Maud Wall and them fallen girls all knowing it. I could maybe look bad in front of a lot of people unless I did some fancy talking and made it out to be some kind of great sheriffing, which was what my mind was chewing on even as I swallowed elk. Them people on the one hand, and all them ranchers, Bark and all, on the other. Them and half of White Sulphur, wanting prosperity. And no way to please a one of them or anchor down votes or do any favors.

But worst of all was Hook. He was the cause of it all. He was pure stubborn. If he'd just bend a little it'd all get fixed up fine. An old fellow like him holding up the whole county. I hated that man, no two ways about it.

Funny the way he fills a room. He's shorter than me, maybe seventy pounds lighter and frail-looking. But he walks in quiet and no one's disrespectful of him. Not ever. Not like with me. I try to get along nice with folk and the next thing I know, that Wall woman is calling me venal and Sam Hook is calling me a fat errand boy right to my face. I'll get him for that some day. And even old drunk Harp toys with me like some dog. And that's not all, neither. Bark and them ranchers, they bring me out there just to tell me off and dismiss me, just like that.

The dinner fixed me up some, my carcass anyway, but my spirits were hitting bottom, so I signaled the barkeep — him and me were the only ones in there late afternoon — and he brought me a bottle of corn spirits, a beaker, and a little water pitcher, same as always, and I poured a stiff one to balm the tired from me.

That Hook, all he seemed to do was stand on his rights, quietlike. When he said something you always knew he meant it and wasn't blowing no smoke. And if there was trouble that he couldn't get around, he didn't run, neither — like maybe he wasn't afraid to die; like he had lived with death a long time and almost didn't care. So he'd give his word and it was always good, and he'd defend his rights and not give a hoot what others thought. Like the only thing he cared about was what he thought of himself, or maybe what his Maker thought of him. He was living easy with himself is all. Not that he scorned others or their respect, but he didn't go hunting it down and didn't need to be liked.

I sighed and poured another. The belly-fire felt good. I was getting so I loathed myself and maybe some spirits would help. Me, I tried to help people out and do favors and I got treated worse than a dog. I liked wearing the star and walking down the streets with my six-gun showing and people always polite and a little careful around me. I liked that and I liked keeping the peace in a nice town with a bright future. But I couldn't stand myself no more — that rotten feeling I got, especially with Hook eyeing me. The sick feeling in my gut never went away now, and I didn't like looking people in the eye for fear they'd see me.

I downed the glass and poured.

Molly sat down, coming from somewhere, and looked at me strange. The place was still nearly empty.

"Something's eating you. I haven't seen you hitting the bottle like this for a year," she said.

I studied her some. She was a strong one. A little steamy, sort of. Kind and friendly one day and a catamount the next.

"I'm a whore," I said. "I don't deserve this star."

She smiled. "Lots of people are whores, Will. It's one way of surviving."

"Not the best way."

"Sometimes there is no other way. And you're not alone, Will. Some of those people who live on the hill and wouldn't give me the time of day are the worst whores of all. A whore is just someone who's sold out something. Some of my girls are whores and some aren't."

"I'm one," I said. "I ain't got nothing inside me. I'm just bought and sold. I ain't a man. Gave up being a man," I mumbled.

She paused a moment. "I got hot girls and cold," she said at last. "The hot girls like it. They can hardly wait . . . they have fun. I was a hot one when I was flatbacking. I always had a fine time, except for once in a while when I had a mean one or a crazy. The hot ones, they're not really whores. I got some cold ones, and they're the whores. They hate it. They cringe inside and want it over with fast, and just do it because they have to. They're the whores."

I nodded. "I'm hot and cold both," I said. "But Molly, I'll tell you something and don't you never repeat it. I'd give up this here shiny star in a minute if I could be a man, be treated like a man. If I knew I was a man, the way Hook knows he's a man.

All I got is a damned tin star."

Her eyes were soft.

"We can't help being what we are," she said quietly. "We get pushed into things by life and whatever happens. Do you think I grew up in Joplin wanting to run a cathouse? You think the girls that come here dreamed of being whores when they grew up? They got into this life to survive. It beat starving and dying, or getting beaten up. Only a few are happy in it, but it's a living, food and a warm bed and friends. I think life pushes a man, too, but maybe differently because you got more choices. Even so, by the time you're twenty, you're stuck with what you got. I mean, the way you are, the way you conduct yourself. That shouldn't happen. Maybe when you're forty or fifty, but not twenty. You get dealt a hand by twenty, and you men have got to play it."

"I got jokers and deuces," I muttered. My head buzzed.

"You've got to survive any which way," she said. "You got a right to survive any way you can."

"Hook survives, and he's maybe seventy. And he survives his own way, not any which way, neither."

"Hook's a man," she said.

71

I swallowed a big gulp, my head pulsed, and I felt like crying. Molly, she just stared sadly at me, stood up, and left me there, hanging.

CHAPTER 6

I kept thinking about Widow Thwait's golden oak two-hundred-dollar box. It didn't make no sense if no one needed planting.

I figgered I'd better mosey on over there and see whether someone croaked, or was going to, or whether she just planted petunias in it, or maybe buried a pet goat. She was a strange one.

I set the bay at an easy jog and rolled over the plank bridge, south and west, toward the Thwait place. She wasn't so far off, and I'd be back early. I was still mad at Jethro so I didn't say nothing. I just took off and left White Sulphur without a sheriff for a few hours. They had a town marshal anyway.

The Thwait place on the Deep Creek road to Helena wasn't very good pasture country, the way I heard it. Not much water over there and the land all bare and full of sagebrush and tilted on end. Old Man Thwait never made much of a go of it before the dropsy took him off three years ago. First thing after planting him she sold the bony longhorns and bought black Angus but they turned out just as bony. The cattle buyers, though, wanted Herefords or Angus, or the black and whiteface cross, so maybe she done the right thing. But she never got paid much for her light steers, breed or no breed, and the story was that she brooded upon it, all alone out there except for her two hands, the ancient Kid Dunham and the young Leonard Carroll.

The worse things got for her, the more she took to blaming Hook and his big skinny longhorns. Last I heard she was in real trouble, and Clay Cott was holding off foreclosing for a final year, mostly out of pity. But he was charging her an extra two percent for being a poor risk, and he had papers on her herd so she couldn't sell or buy or do nothing without his say-so. That's the way of banks, since before I was born, I figgered. Pretty soon he'd have it, unless she come up with something. Funny she got them double eagles for the box.

It was a bright day, but there was a mean wind whipping off of Canada so I had the hood up and the isinglass windows unrolled, and was tolerably fine in there. It beat forking a horse for certain.

I'd find out about the box and maybe wangle some guest privileges and a meal — not that Mary Ellen Thwait was any sort of cook. The fact is, she wore man-duds and cooked no better. But she could dish up a half-decent dinner if she was of a mind. And maybe I'd get to stay in the guest room if I strung it right. You never know about them widows and their needs, so I figgered I'd just sort of make some opportunity and see which way the cowpie fell.

The outfit was down in a long swale with nary a tree in sight, except for some cottonwoods around the small spring that watered the home place. It was a bleak land, long boned and grazed bare anywhere near water. The board-and-batt house and shed were paintless but some sign of ancient whitewash still clung to the silvered planking.

I clambered down and left the six-gun on the seat so as not to alarm anybody. No one was visible although the whimpering wind made it sound like there was a nursery full of squalling babies.

She was waiting quiet at the door, gray eyes focused on me steady.

"State your business, Sheriff," she said toughlike with no welcome in it.

"Just visiting," I said. "Making the rounds. Thought you'd have some coffee on the range."

"Suit yourself. Pot's on the edge. Push it center a little for warming up."

She followed me in and I headed for the

kitchen. But it was the parlor that caught my eye as I passed the door. The box was in there. On sawhorses. With some candles lit and some black bunting dragged around and the shades all drawn. I pretended like I didn't see nothing and poured a mugful from the speckled blue enamel pot.

I sipped a little and then got down to it. Widow Thwait was not one for beating around the bush.

"Someone die?" I asked. "Jasper Jethro said he delivered a box."

"No, no, not yet," she replied. "But soon."

"One of your hands? Old Dunham?"

"No."

"Some stranger? Peddler?"

"No."

"You mind telling me?"

She smiled suddenly and her pasty, pinched face relaxed.

"Sam Hook," she said. "I'm just celebrating in advance so when I kill him I'll get double the pleasure out of it. Come on in and make yourself to home. I'll show you."

We went on into the parlor and there it was, the golden oak glinting in the candlelight and the tapers flaming in banked rows.

"Pretty impressive," I said. "You're celebrating in style, Mary Ellen."

"Sam Hook's gonna lie in there with a bullet hole right between the eyes, and I'll invite all the neighbors in to see," she said. "I'll get him dolled up in his black Sunday best, and wrestle on the celluloid collar and then lay him in there with one eye open and the other eye shut so you can sort of peer inside and see him dead as a doornail, and look into the blue hole in his forehead, too."

"Mary Ellen, you got this here high-priced box for Sam Hook and you're going to shoot him?"

"He doesn't deserve pine. He gets golden oak," she said, lifting the little thirty-thirty saddle carbine sitting there and swinging it slowly past my belly. My palms itched. My scalp tingled too. I sure was distempered by it.

"I'm getting good. Look here." She strode to the open door with all the sunshine of that porchless place, swept the little gun up and blasted a magpie. Black and white feathers exploded and the bird — what was left of it — thunked into the clay.

"Getting good," she repeated absently as she flipped back the bolt and popped a new shell into the chamber while the old clattered on the plank floor.

I didn't like the cut of this at all and I regretted leaving my six-gun out there in my buggy. I was as unarmed as a polled Hereford in a slaughterhouse. I figgered maybe silence was my best bet.

"Cott's almost got my place and before he does and I go under, Hook's going with me. He did it to me, you know. Him and his Blackfeet Injuns. They come in the night on over Black Butte Mountain, deliberate, and run those dirty longhorns into my good clean Angus. Dirty bulls on my clean heifers. He sneaks in and stands at the foot of my four-poster and laughs at me in the night. I can hardly stand the sight of it."

I smiled some. "Why's he do that?"

"He hates me. Been plotting this for years to get even."

"You talk to Ham Bark about it? About Hook running his longhorn bulls, middle of the night, into your broodstock?"

She glanced at me sideways. "No, I haven't. And I never will. He's in with them. Once they get me down, Ham Bark's going to buy up this place for a song from Clay Cott."

"How you know that?"

She stared at me coldly. "How do you think? It's plain as day, what's happening."

"What do your hands, Carroll and Dunham, think about it?"

She gave me a crafty look. "I've said nothing

to them. They're in the middle of this too, you know."

She was waving that thirty-thirty around a little wild and I was sweating even though it was tomb-cold in there. I was wanting to ask where she figgered to place me in it but I got smart and didn't, for fear it'd start something.

"You got some good apple pie for a hungry sheriff?" I asked, and tried to laugh lightsomely.

She kind of squinted at me and quietlike set down that popgun and headed for the kitchen.

"Not apple," she said. "You crazy? Apples in May? I got a canned peach one half eaten up."

"I've come a long way," I said cheerily. "Guess I'll wash up and then dig in."

I grinned and, feeling a little shaky, wobbled out to my buggy and slid the six-gun belt on. Then I went down to the horse trough to splash my face good. I had some thinking to do, and fast.

When I got back to the kitchen, the canned-peach pie was waiting.

"Mary Ellen," I said after I dug into my second slice, "them hands of yours. Are you keeping them busy and all?"

"Mr. Thwait directs them," she said simply.

I ignored that about her late husband and asked, "They come in every night and report to you, do they? They stay over in that bunk-house, do they?"

"Every night. And they see to my needs every morning. After that they begin to work for Mr. Thwait, just as always."

"They bring you tallies and all, and drive the herds into the pens here for a lookover, and do the cutting and the doctoring and the winter feeding? They put up hay?"

"They tell me they do. They tell me Mr. Thwait is very satisfied with their work."

"What'd Carroll say when you sent him into White Sulphur for that box?"

"Why, nothing. He did it, is all."

"Did you tell him your intentions? Planting Sam Hook in it, I mean?"

"Of course not. That isn't their business."

"Now tell me again what you're planning for old Hook. When are you going to get him?"

"Why, I shall shoot him between the eyes and put him in the box and hold a brief memorial service with proper readings and then bury him."

"Here or on his spread?"

"Here. I'll bury him proper here, and with a good stone marker."

"Now tell me again why."

"Why? Because he deserves it. Like Mr. Thwait did."

I sputtered some over my java.

"What would you think," I ventured, "of selling out and coming on into White Sulphur to live, Mary Ellen? Nice little whitewashed cottage in town; friendly folk to see every day. There may be enough here in land and stock and all to satisfy Clay and get you fixed up nice."

"You're one of them," she replied. "Mr. Thwait warned against longhorns. No. I'll stay here and shoot Sam Hook and his big skinny beeves, then things will get better. You'll see. And you, Sheriff Oglesby, are corrupting yourself trying to steal land from a poor widow."

"Now, now, Mary Ellen. I was just coming to look after you and maybe win your support and vote next November."

"Women can't vote," she retorted. "And you're an ass."

She'd picked up that carbine again and I sort of wiggled out of there fastlike.

"Thanks for the delicious apricot pie, Mary Ellen," I yelled.

"Canned peach," she yelled back.

I whipped the bay around and settled him into his easy jog. I rode east betwixt great slabs of prairie, sloping so long I couldn't see the mountains except now and then. In the Smith River valley there was a fork in the road. I could head north and on up the North Fork to White Sulphur in easy time for a good hot supper. Or I could start the long hard drive south to Sixteen Mile and warn Hook. I wouldn't even get there until evening, and then I'd have a long night-ride home because Hook wouldn't have me on his place. I pulled up at the fork and pondered it some. The bay wanted to head home and get his snootful of oats. But I turned him south, feeling crazy because Hook could take care of himself and didn't need no warnings from me.

The days were long, it being early May, and there was still daylight when I wheeled in there. The Injun Padlock materialized spooklike out of nowhere and I told him I was just staying a minute, so to leave the bay alone.

The old man was sitting quiet in a rocker on that long covered porch, enjoying the twilight, I guess. I could see his white handlebar twitch as I approached.

"What's your business, Oglesby?" he asked coldly.

"That's twice I've been asked that today," I began. "I'll just take a minute and be on my way. I been up to visit with Widow Thwait and find out how come she bought a box from Jasper Jethro. . . ."

Then, simple and direct as I knew how, I told him the whole business: the box and candles, the threats against him, which I described in detail, and all.

As Hook listened quietly in the dusk, his eyes were gentle, not boring in on me like usual. I finished and there was a stretching silence.

"Why did you drive all the way down here?" he asked.

"I figgered it was my duty."

"You looking for my vote next November?"

"No, I never thought of it," I answered truthfully.

"Nice of you to let me know. I've never had to deal with a crazed woman. I don't rightly see how to defend myself . . ."

That was his roundabout way of acknowledging the unwritten law of the frontier — you don't kill women. Not ever.

"Well, I'd better be off to White Sulphur —," I began.

He stayed me. "Have you had any grub?" he asked.

"Not rightly. Just that pie."

"I'll have Padlock rustle up a meal. There's some cold haunch and some beans."

"That'd be neighborly."

"Set a spell, Oglesby."

I did, settling into the other rocker there in the velvet dusk. The air was tender. Some audacious early stars winked.

We sat silent a long time, seems like.

"Something I don't understand," he said after a while, "perhaps you can enlighten me. Why did you come here?"

He left the rest unsaid, the part about the long detour and the seven-hour haul I was facing. But he was staring at me, all intent. I could feel it more than see it.

Something sort of clobbered up in my throat and made me hoarse.

"See this here shiny star? I ain't much. I ain't very worthy of it. Maybe it's too late for a fellow like me to change. But I got to the fork and the star was saying to me, Do your duty for once. So I done it. And I ain't apologizing."

He didn't say nothing, but the silence coming from him was good. After a bit that Padlock showed up in the door.

"Your chow's on the table, Mr. Oglesby," said Sam Hook. "Go on in and eat. If you don't mind, I'll just sit there. And if you're not in a rush, stay over. There's a bunk off the kitchen. We'll grain the bay and you can ride up to town rested in the morning."

"I'm obliged," I replied.

I dug into them good vittles at the big plank table, wiped my face good afterward, and when I was getting up it sort of hit me.

He'd called me mister.

CHAPTER 7

I hadn't gotten an hour away from Hook's place the next morning when that young buck Jerome, Hook's nephew, rose up out of some chokecherry beside the rutted road and stopped me. He gave me a fright, and I was grabbing for the six-gun until I saw who it was.

"Come," he said. "We've caught them red-handed, if an Indian may use that expression, and you can make the arrests."

I didn't like the sound of that, but I didn't have no choice. I set the brake, bush-tied the bay, buckled on the artillery, and set off shanks' mare behind the Injun, who was on a tough little mustang. By the time we'd climbed half a mile up a brush-filled coulee, I was wheezing and full of belly sweat. Some people sweat in the head, but I sweat around the breastbone and down over the gut. That six-gun bouncing on my thigh was no joy neither. But I said nothing.

And then we come on them. About fifty yards apart were sprawled two dead longhorn bulls, one a gaunt brindle and the other a stringy gray. Ugly damn things. I seen Hook's fishhook brand plain as day on both, and the blood still dripping from a couple of holes in each.

Standing there with arms sky high were two people I sure didn't want to see, Strunck and Kratz. Them two hardcases were about as ornery as any in Meagher County. Strunck was a giant, almost seven feet of bone and sinew, and one of those carrot-type redheads with mean green eyes. Kratz was just plain big, but not an ounce of fat in it, and with a voice so low it bellied out of the earth. He was auburn-haired and fat-nosed. Holding them quiet was Padlock, staring from under his black derby with flat black eyes, his Winchester steady as a jail bar. He was quiet, the way a catamount on a limb is quiet, and even them two wildmen knew they were an inch from dead.

Jerome picked up his Winchester and I sort of felt it was pointing half at me and half at them two paid toughs of Stern and Monk. I didn't like it none, so I filled my hand with iron, in case there were any jokers here. I scanned the brush, looking for hidden trouble.

"Get these damn bucks off us, 'fore I kill them and you," snarled Strunck.

Padlock's flat black eyes just grew flatter and

the barrel moved toward Strunck's breastbone.

"Check his Spencer," said Padlock quietly like he had every right in the world to hand out orders to a white man.

But it made sense, so I went over to the repeater that was lying on the turf. I was careful not to step into the crossfire. I hoisted the gun up and yanked the bolt; sure enough there was an empty in the chamber and the fresh stink of saltpeter and sulphur. The magazine was one short when I slid all them brass cartridges out.

Them Injuns sure had the goods on that pair. There were flyers on both Kratz and Strunck, trouble a yard long. Most recent incident was over to Miles City where the pair had preyed on immigrants. I'd known about them for a long time but I didn't do nothing because the Stern and Monk outfit was nothing to trifle with. But now I was stuck with that pair of deuces, who looked ready to rush me, Injun bullets or not.

"We was framed. Arrest them Injuns for shooting bulls, damn their red hides," Kratz demanded. "You don't do it, I'll pound your fat brains out."

I sighed. "Them are Hook's nephew and brother-in-law."

"I don't care if they're his auntie and grandmother. You get them and let us white men go – or I'll gouge your eyes and slice your tongue and cut off your ears, Oglesby."

It seemed like Jerome's bore pointed a little more at Kratz's nose.

I turned to Padlock. "Whyn't you boys put them guns down and let me handle this?" I grinned, but the Injuns just squinted.

"As sheriff, I'm ordering you: put them guns down or get arrested. I'll handle it now."

"I think not," said Padlock. He just stood there.

I was in a sweat. Even if the Injuns turned the pair over to me, taking them two all the way to White Sulphur would be as tough a thing as I'd ever done. (I only had one pair of cuffs and they were back in the buggy.) But that was just the beginning of it: I'd be in hot water not only with Stern and Monk, but the whole rancher bunch, and maybe lose their support. Or worse. I didn't like their threats and I didn't doubt for a minute that they'd do what they said they would. I was going to have to wiggle out of this somehow.

"I don't see that they done anything," I said to Padlock. "It's just your say-so against theirs. Not much good in court."

"Indian testimony doesn't count for much in your courts," Padlock replied so quiet and civil

I had to strain to hear him. "But your court will accept the testimony of crooked sheriffs, as long as they are white."

I boiled up so mad I was near speechless. And just then Kratz saw his chance and made a move. Next I knew he was toppling over like a sawed-off cottonwood and I seen old Hook himself knocking Kratz senseless with the butt of his gun. Strunck, he was bulling toward Hook but the old man swung catlike and Strunck stopped short, then went white when he saw them bores and the look in Hook's eye.

"I'll kill you, Hook," he snarled.

It seemed to me I'd heard enough death threats in the last few days to fill a star-packing lifetime.

Hook nodded to Jerome who lifted a mess of thong from his possibles and tied up them two bullshooters.

"Well?" said Sam Hook.

"Now see here," I began, thinking fast. "I ain't exactly got much evidence that them two shot your bulls. It could've been a frame-up like they said, something you rigged up. I don't want trouble. . . ."

Hook didn't say nothing.

". . . I think maybe I'll just take these two fellas on over to Stern and Monk and have them pick up their duds and get out of the county. Does that suit you?"

Hook just grinned through his mustache. "Rustling's a hanging offense," he said.

"Who said anything about rustling? There ain't no rustling."

"Those bulls look awfully rustled to me. They could hardly be more rustled."

"Now see here —"

"They'll hang," said that crazy old loon, them two barrels inadvertently and carelessly pointing at me.

"I'll have you on murder, Hook —"

He just nodded quietlike, while Jerome was uncoiling hemp. Kratz was coming around and groaning. He shook away the cobwebs and stared at Jerome.

"You hang me and I'll kill you," Kratz muttered. Strunck went gray.

Jerome, lithe as a cat, flipped the lariat over the limb of a big ponderosa, the only tree in a mile. It was almost as if God had planted that tree there for the hanging of Lorenzo Strunck and Dale Kratz.

Truth to tell, shooting them bulls was rustling all right, both by law and by the custom of the folk here. Hook was well within his rights. But dammit, if he did it, all hell would bust loose. At least maybe. I figgered Strunck and Kratz were wanted men, five or six murder counts and a mess of robberies and more flyers

91

in my office than I could count. First-rate bandits, maybe even celebrity types like Billy the Kid. Maybe if I took their carcasses back to White Sulphur and let folks know what I done, with a little help from some ranchers down here, I'd be sheriff for just about life.

I beamed. "Let's get at it."

"I want a legal trial," Strunck muttered.

"You just got one. You're guilty as sin," I retorted.

Hook said, "That's what I figured."

Jerome had the rope over the limb now and was leading in a black and a sorrel from the brush down below.

"Who's first?" Hook asked.

"I am," yelled Kratz. "Get rid of my headache."

"Anything you want to say? Want to confess? Want a prayer? Anyone you want notified?"

"No."

"All right then."

Jerome pried open the thong around Kratz's calves. The giant redhead stood up shaky, but calm. He'd die like a man I figgered. He shrugged off help and managed to step into the saddle even with his hands lashed behind him.

"I hate this," said Sam Hook. "I hate it right down to my bowels."

"Then why —?"

He fixed me with them hazel eyes. "They earned it in Miles from what I hear. And rustling's a capital offense. And it may stop the slaughter of my stock."

Jerome led the black to the tree, dropped the noose over Kratz's neck, and pulled it up solid. Then he drew the hemp taut and tied it off. Kratz just hunkered down.

Jerome glanced up at Hook. Hook nodded. Jerome slapped the rump of the black. The horse bolted. Kratz dropped through air and bounced with a savage crack. He flopped wildly a moment, then sagged. Strunck puked. Hook stood sad and calm. I walked uphill until my belly settled. When I turned around Kratz was on the ground and Jerome was sliding off the hemp.

"He died easy," I muttered.

"No one dies easily," Hook growled.

There was a kind of thunder up on the horizon and five or six horsemen boiled over and rattled down. I glanced around some. Padlock was disappearing into the thick brush, Jerome was grabbing his carbine, and Hook was just standing there with his two-barrel resting on the sorrel's saddle, aimed right into the riders. Then I seen it was Bark — I could spot that orange face way off, and it looked to be Stern and Monk too, and some of their hands. I recognized Bark's foreman Winfrid Coop. They wheeled up and spread out, half surrounding us. They were blackfaced and breathing fire as they spotted Kratz and the noose and Strunck tied up.

"What the hell," Bark growled, his old Army Colt out and waving.

"You've strung Kratz," Stern shouted.

"Rustling. As you can see." Hook said it nonchalantly.

"What do you mean, rustling. I see two dead bulls is what I see," Bark said.

"Rustling," replied Hook. "I've had twelve bulls rustled I know of. Probably more. It's a capital offense. As you know. Always has been."

He kind of had them there, I figgered.

"They weren't rustling; they were shooting your damned bulls. Now you killed him for nothing and you're going to hang for it, Hook."

Sam Hook shrugged. "Rustling. How many times have you and the rest of the district ranchers strung up some hardcases you caught with a dead steer?"

"That's different," Bark howled. "That's totally different."

"You're right, Hamilton. The difference is that this time you or Stern or Monk gave the orders and the hardcases were rustling for the brand."

"You accusing me —"

"Oh, sure, yes. You're in the middle of it. The rustling." Sam Hook's eyes were gentle.

"Now, Sam, this ain't rustling and you know it," argued Monk. "This is just ranchwork, cleaning out scrubs is what, and now you've murdered one of my best and most trusted hands who was going to be my foreman soon. And we barely saved Strunck here. We saw Oglesby's buggy parked over the hump and the tracks and we came up to help him with whatever it was."

Hook eyed me. "Tell them," he said.

"Tell what?"

"Recite a little history of this Strunck and Kratz."

"I don't know nothing," I mumbled. "Just a couple of Wyoming drovers I guess."

Hook laughed sardonically through his bristling mustache.

I didn't like this mess none. Them others were spread out fighter style. Winfrid Coop was no one to mess with, I knew, and the rest had their carbines or revolvers in hand, picking targets among Jerome, Hook and me.

"Take Strunck and tell him to get out of the Territory or I'll come after him," Hook said. "From now on, all rustlers of my beeves get strung up."

95

"Fetch him, Ray," Stern directed. A tough kid, maybe sixteen and swaggering, jumped down, cut Strunck loose, and helped him onto his sorrel.

"Take Kratz," Hook said, "unless Oglesby here wants him."

"Why should I want him?" I asked indignant.

"Then take him and plant him nice," Hook said to Monk but giving me an evil look.

I could see Bark stewing up there on his stallion, getting orange again, and that meant trouble.

"Now see here, Hook. You think you're getting away with this? We're taking you in for murder and we're going to string up that thieving buck of yours." The six-gun was leveled now. "Drop it, Hook."

Then it seemed like all them flopping carbines got sort of pointed, most on Hook, and one or two on Jerome. Hook stood still as granite. That shotgun, I don't know quite how something moves unseen, but it was pointing right back at Bark and at Stern too, who was in the line of fire beyond Bark.

"Drop it, Hook, or I'll shoot," Bark roared. "There's five other guns on you."

Hook just smiled. "I'd like you to meet my nephew Jerome," he said.

Jerome said, "How do you do? I'm pleased to

meet you." His carbine, leveled on Monk, didn't budge an inch.

Bark stared down into them black holes of Hook's and started to sweat. I seen the water bead up on his brow and then pour out all over his face and bare skull.

It got tense around there, and I eased back slowly, trying to get out of the line of fire if it blew. I was in the middle of hell-on-earth, I figgered. But mostly I was just watching Bark sweat while Hook stood there collected as ever.

Bark finally broke the spell. "Disarm that Injun," he said to Winfrid Coop, and Coop started to do it.

"Don't," I yelled.

Monk said, "Keep your fat gut out of this, Oglesby."

Hook, his eyes riveted on Bark, simply stepped forward. Then he took another step. And another. And Bark just let him, sweat oozing out. Hook just walked up until he was six or eight feet from Bark, that shotgun never wavering, walking into the barrel of Bark's six-gun until they were both point blank. I never seen nothing like it, Hook walking into that six-gun and Bark sweating and staring down into them two black holes. I'll remember that as long as I live. It was as if the old man didn't care if he lived or died.

"Kill that Injun, Winfrid," rasped Bark.

"Don't," I yelled. "They got an ace. The other buck, he's in that brush somewheres with his repeater and by the time you figger where he is, three or four of us will be meat."

Bark was running rivulets, but then he began to pink out and I knew it was over. Slowlike, he lowered his old Colt and holstered it, and the tension seemed to drain away.

"You treed us this time, Hook, but it doesn't mean much. You're alone. We'll get you. You and those thieving Blackfeet will be stretching hemp before long. And after we finish off your bulls, we'll start on your cows, and then your steers, and then your calves until there's nothing left."

"Take Kratz and get out," Hook replied.

Bark addressed me: "Go on back to White Sulphur and forget about this. I mean forget. We told you to stay out of here and you came sticking your nose in. Do it again and you'll disappear. Lots of accidents happen down here."

That riled me, addressing the Meagher County sheriff like that. I lit out of there and didn't feel a bit at ease until I got down to the buggy on the Smith River road and collapsed into the quilted seat.

CHAPTER 8

The next morning Hook rode into town and by noon all hell had busted loose. I seen the roan in Tin's livery but didn't pay no attention to it until lunchtime when half the nabobs, moguls, and leading lights of White Sulphur came stomping into my jailhouse.

I peered up at that sea of black gabardine and boiled collars and I knew something was up. Among them worthies was Jeff Bark, banging his gold-knobbed walking stick on the jail floor; Clay Cott, squinting at me pig-eyed from behind his banker jowls; Clyde Park, the gaunt hollow-cheeked albino lawyer who handled the county's legal business on the side; Marvin Capp, the dry-goods man; and of course Jethro, who never missed out on anything.

Jeff Bark led off: "We've a notice for you to hand to Hook. He's over at the Sherman Hotel taking lunch — or rather, trying to take lunch. They're refusing to serve him because he's got that Blackfeet buck with him. And Maud Wall too."

"What's the notice for?" I asked.

"A competence hearing. If I find he's got senile dementia we'll pop him off to Warm Springs."

I grinned easy. "He's crazy as a loon, I could testify to that."

"Well, see that you do," Jeff Bark said. "Your job depends on it. Now get to it."

"Whoa up. Now what's this all about? How come I'm doing this here?"

Judge Bark grimaced. He was a toothy man, and when he spoke his molars clacked and clicked. "This morning Harry Alter came busting into the middle of a chicken-stealing trial and beckoned me. So I recessed and met him in chambers. 'Jeff,' he whispered, 'Hook came into the clerk office to record a deed. He's turned the whole ranch, kit and caboodle, over to a partnership composed of Maud Wall and those two Indians of his. He ain't got an acre left to his name.'

"That was crazy enough, but only the beginning. The old man's on a rampage. Clay, you tell your side of it."

The banker sighed and slipped a Doan's Liver Pill onto his sticky tongue. "The next thing Hook did, as far as any of us can tell, was storm into my office, walking right past the teller and through the wooden gate and all.

'Clay,' he said, 'this bank leaks like a sieve. I'm closing my account and transferring to Helena. And I'll take it in gold.' Now I couldn't imagine what he meant by that: we have a sterling reputation of service to all, the great and humble – and of course total confidentiality, as well.

"Well, I argued with him some, and of course I told him we didn't have that much specie here and he'd have to take a draft. He just said – well, I shan't repeat it in polite company, but he referred to the offal of a bull. I told him he was making a tragic mistake, and an ill-considered move, and that he hadn't given it mature deliberation the way an established and fine rancher should. And of course I told him he was hurting the town and the valley, and I urged him to take a draft, a cashier's check, but he would have none of it, and just used that language not fit for polite company. So I finally went over to the safe and doled it out to him in double eagles, and he just grinned at me as if to tell me I hadn't been speaking truth – a most evil grin I must say – and technically he was right, but I was just trying to keep that poor crazy fellow from walking out of there unarmed and old and vulnerable with all that gold. But he put it in a big leather saddlebag and slung it over his shoulder – heavy, y'know, gold is heavy — and walked out straight as a ramrod, not even saying goodbye. I felt so sad, seeing a man decompose before my very eyes."

I turned to Clyde Park, standing there all white and smart-alecky, although I'd never say that to him to his face.

"I seemed to be next in Hook's rampage," Park began in a brittle, tissuepaper voice. "He just barged in and accused me, uh ... he questioned some aspects of the confidentiality of our lawyer-client relationship, and of course I denied that any such breach ever occurred, but he wasn't really listening. Then he asked me to draw up an agreement, right on the spot, turning the livestock over to the three above-mentioned parties but reserving to himself the right to manage his establishment until he died or voluntarily relinquished control.

"And of course I replied, 'My dear old man and friend, have you carefully considered this rash act?' And so on, and of course I declined to do what he asked, for his sake. He is without issue and his estate must be protected from people such as — well, you understand. And I, as his good steward, was compelled to refuse his request. Of course I suggested that the character of the three parties be publicly examined first, and so on, but he would have none of it. And then, sad to say, he discharged me as his counselor and bade me return certain papers, which I did most reluctantly, knowing his present state of mental disintegration. Worse, he announced most vindictively that he would retain that old lush Harp. Imagine it, Harp! Harp as counsel for a great enterprise! Of course then I knew that senility was ravaging him and the good old fellow needed the protection of the Territory and its magistrates. So of course I consulted Judge Bark about a competency hearing, and notice to Hook, and a date for it, and so forth. . . ."

I was blotting up all that when Jethro began squeaking and flapping. "And that's not all, Will," said Jethro. "He's sitting there, bold as you please, in Clifton Smoot's fancy dining salon with that buck Padlock and Maud Wall. Clifton tells him right off, no Indians served, but Sam Hook just sits there, crazylike with the others, and says he'll wait for lunch. And Smoot says he'll wait all afternoon. And now Harp's with them too, and Smoot beckoned me over to the lobby and told me to fetch you to kick out that Blackfeet or he'd file a complaint, disturbing the peace, or trespass, or whatever."

"That poor old man's lost his mind, obviously," summed up Judge Bark. "We must help him. Here's the notice, Will. Soon as I hold the hearing in two weeks and find that he's slipped into senile dementia, we can undo this morning's damage . . . and a lot of other damage done to the county and its merchants over the last two years."

I didn't want to serve no summons on that old bearcat.

"This a summons?" I asked.

"No. Just a notice. He has the right to attend the hearing, but it's not required and this isn't a criminal action," explained County Attorney Park. "We're required to let him know."

"And of course we want this to be a proceeding beyond reproach," Bark added.

Well, I hung on my heavy six-shooter and we trooped on over to the Sherman Hotel, a red brick monster that jutted into Main Street because of some mismatched town plats and forced traffic to swerve around it.

Hook was there, all right, sitting right under the fancy cutglass chandelier in that flossy dining room. Along with Padlock, and Maud Wall, and Francis Harp. The snowy linen cloth at their table had nothing on it but the tables of all them other lunchers in the place were heaped with plates and chow.

I figgered we must have looked like a platoon of crows or maybe magpies, all of us in black suits. Well, that's the way the town's leading citizens ought to look. Dignified.

"Gentlemen, pull up some chairs," said Sam Hook.

"Naw, we'll just be here a moment," I replied. "Got something for you, Sam."

He glanced quizzically at me and took the proffered sheet. After studying the notice some, he handed it to Harp. "Seems I'm to be the guest of honor at my lunching," he said quietly.

Harp passed it along to Padlock and Maud. The buck, he pulled out some gold-rimmed cheaters to read it.

"This party will be held in a forthnight, eh?" asked Harp. "A gala affair it will be. Shall we supply the violinist, Sam?"

Sam Hook grinned. And I caught that darned Maud staring at me cat-eyed again.

"These things require a preacher," said Harp. "There must be a benediction and an opening prayer. I shall invite the Reverend Mr. House. And you, Jefferson, shall bring the ice cream and cookies."

Judge Bark rapped his cane sharply, but unfortunately this wasn't no court. Me, I just barged ahead.

"Now I got another matter. Smoot's complaining. You know there's no Injuns served in here. You got to get out now. Either that or Padlock's got to wait outside or I'll have you all booked for disturbing the peace. Smoot's yelling trespass, too."

"My, my imagine that," said Francis Harp. "Disturbing the peace." He gazed around the crowded hall. "The place is plainly in an uproar," he said.

"Gentlemen," said Sam Hook, "I'd like you to meet Mr. Padlock, my brother-in-law and one of the valley's leading cattlemen and pioneers."

I'll say this for old Bark and all. They just stared and didn't lift a paw. Me, I figgered a man's a man, and I shook hands with that Injun.

"Delighted to meet you, gentlemen," said Padlock. "We shall leave. I wouldn't want to disturb Mr. Smoot's peace."

Hook stood.

"Well then," he said, "this seems to be the day to take my trade elsewhere."

He grinned that strange grin of his at Clyde Park and Clay Cott, and them two just stood there, uncomfortable and purple-faced.

So the bunch of us sauntered out onto the verandah, all us black crows, the buck in his black bowler and red calico, Maud in her navy linen dress, and Hook with his big gray John B. Stetson shading that bristly mustache. Them other crows, they looked pained and sort of skittered off soon as they hit daylight. They didn't much like being made fun of by Harp and Hook. I was about to cut loose when Hook laid a hand on my shoulder.

"Still the errand boy, Oglesby?"

"Just legal business," I retorted stiffly.

"Come along with us. We'll lunch at Molly's."

"Sam!" cried Maud. "That's unthinkable. I shall not."

Sam replied, "Where else can Padlock eat? You name the place and we'll go to it."

She paused, helplessly.

"Molly would be delighted to serve him, especially now that he's one of our leading citizens."

Padlock, he just grinned.

Maud looked doubtful, and glanced eastward toward her home. But then Hook extended his arm, she took it and clenched in close, and off we went.

"It's high noon, Maud. The soiled doves are all slumbering in their cribs. You'll be accompanied by no less than the sheriff of Meagher County and your distinguished attorney Mr. Harp."

I kind of perked up at that, and Harp smiled lazily.

So we sauntered on over there, past the hot spring purling out sulphur water, and into Molly's first-floor saloon. Maud's eyes were big as billiard balls, taking it all in, but when she saw there were no naked ladies or nothing like that around, she sort of unclenched from old Hook. I seen something then. I seen in her face that she loved him, and he loved her. It was scribbled over them two. She was doing it — dining in a cathouse — *for him*, because of his say-so; and it made that old face of hers danged near pretty. In fact, real pretty.

"I shall have a sarsaparilla," muttered Francis Harp as he eyed the whiskey bottles flirtatiously.

Molly was nowhere in sight; probably hadn't gotten out of her four-poster spring-mattress flouncy-covered bed yet. But that Chinese cook, he soon had a heap of good vittles weighing down our table. Maud relaxed some, but not entire, and she kept eyeing the door as if she expected God himself to walk in and catch her.

Padlock dug in, and he had nice manners for an Injun, eating proper with a knife and fork and all. Hook didn't touch much, ate light the way thin old men do. Harp diddled his food around some, mostly enjoying the sight of them fine bottles ranked behind the bar like little soldiers. Nobody said nothing. I figgered that was on account of my being there. They likely would've said a lot away from my ears. It was odd eating silentlike with three crazy people.

After we finished I expected Sam Hook to brace me some way or other, but it turned out to be Francis Harp done it.

"My dear Sheriff," he began, sort of courtly. "You've been running errands, shall we say, for some of the leading lights of the town and valley."

Courtly or not, he steamed me up fast.

"And of course if you can run errands for one group of worthies, you can ran errands for another."

I was sure getting sore.

"My lovely client here, Mrs. Wall, recounted in the most precise detail her, ah, encounter, with you. She has a remarkable mind. A bear trap of a mind. Of course, among those topics which she perfectly recalled was your little aside to her that a cabal of the valley's luminaries was intent upon declaring Mr. Hook incompetent."

Them were big words he used, but I was getting the drift of it.

"Now it doesn't take much imagination to understand why. In a word, greed. Mr. Hook's holdings are large, well run, profitable, and free of encumbrances. His patented land lies exquisitely upon the springs and creeks of the Sixteen Mile country and along Battle Creek as well.

"Nor does it take much imagination to understand the lust that his holdings inspired in the bosom of his former counsel and confidante, Mr. Park, and in the breast of the honorable Judge Bark, and in the heart and soul of the esteemed Mr. Cott.

"Ah, and how exquisitely aware these gentlemen are that Mr. Hook has no children and apparently no close relatives — in short, no heirs. Over the past several years, Mr. Cott has been uncommonly solicitous and has pressed upon Mr. Hook at every opportunity the prospect of refinancing his holdings at most generous terms. Mr. Hook, in his wisdom, has steadily declined. His holdings are free and clear, quite unencumbered by even the most trivial of debts. So the esteemed banker holds no paper of any sort, such as a call loan, that might give the progressive leaders of White Sulphur Springs an opportunity to perform their civic duty and see to it that the great Fishhook Ranch benefits certain individuals upon Sam Hook's demise.

"My dear Mr. Hook here, of course, continues to thwart all this progressive planning not only by persisting in ruddy good health and strong spirit, but also by following his own

110

counsel when it comes to animal husbandry. I refer, of course, to his noble longhorns.

"Ah, my dear Oglesby, you see the issue, of course. What would you do in Sam Hook's place?"

Harp gazed amiably at me. Hook, he was enjoying it. And the way his arm and Maud's disappeared under the table, I figgered the pair of them were holding hands like moonstruck children. As for that Injun, he just gave me that flat-eyed gaze of his, and there was no reading him.

"What Mr. Hook has done, my dear Oglesby, is to render himself nearly penniless. And what you have witnessed today — the transfer of deed at the office of the county clerk, the discharge of the esteemed Clyde Park, and so on — this is the end rather than the beginning of Mr. Hook's changes. He was perfectly aware that an attempt would be made to break his will, that the courts would find reason not to convey his property to persons of the red race. Moreover, the record of his marriage to Mrs. Hook, performed so long ago by that estimable missionary to the Blackfeet and Flatheads, Father de Smet, had long since been destroyed by fire at the mission. And so the Padlocks, father and son, would be hard put to prove their relationship to the, eh, deceased."

Hook smiled amiably, looking rather unde-ceased.

"So a year ago, seeing the way things were heading," continued Harp, "Mr. Hook quietly transferred the bulk of his ranch funds to a trusted Helena bank, and also, through counsel in Helena, created the present partnership and transferred his land and cattle to it, but tarried until now to record the transfer. His will is now a worthless scrap, for there is nothing to pass along.

"So, Honorable Oglesby, your task now is to convey all this juicy gossip to the honorable leaders of White Sulphur, and to suggest that they forget that competency hearing they've scheduled for a fortnight hence. Mr. Hook will retire quietly to his ranch and continue to manage it on behalf of the partnership for as long as he chooses."

"Why, sure, I'll tell them," I said.

Harp smiled lazily and eyed me through half-closed eyes. "And if they should persist in such a hearing, and if they should invite you to testify, what do you plan to say?"

"Why, ah, you can count on me, counselor."

"You are a whore," said Maud Wall.

"See here, ma'am, you shut your yap."

Hook just grinned at me. That grin, that's the sign of a crazy man.

"It is fitting that we have had this kingly repast at Molly's," chimed in Counselor Harp. "Run along now, Honorable Oglesby, and spread the good word."

I beat it out of there, my six-gun banging on my hip, and left them sipping coffee in the cathouse. I beelined straight to Clyde Park's offices, since he was the part-time county attorney, and laid it all out. Park just sat there like an albino Buddha and frowned. But when I finished up, he didn't seem bothered none.

"The joke's on Hook," he said. "The old bird figures he's got it licked. But he doesn't. He's banking on law and order, but that isn't what's going to happen if he should die. Those Blackfeet would get strung up by those hardcase outfits down there about two minutes after Hook's death. And that Wall woman — she'd be forced onto the next stage out of here one way or another. Along with those doxies."

He smiled voluptuously. "It'll all take care of itself, I imagine. There's no reason to suppose Hook will live long. And about two hours after he's buried I'll have court-appointed guardians sitting on that ranch, and his Helena assets frozen with a tax case."

CHAPTER 9

The spring roundup of the Smith River grazing district was fast approaching. Soon the cattlemen, drovers, and reps from all the area ranches would gather and begin to drive the stock down from the remote reaches of the Big Belts to the west, the Little Belts to the north, and the craggy Castle Mountains to the east. At various central points the cattle would be tallied according to their brands, the calves would be weaned, the bullcalves castrated, and the calf crop branded. Some beeves would be culled and shipped.

For a gruelling two or three weeks every rancher and hand in the valley, from the Shields River drainage in the south to the Little Belts north of White Sulphur, would work cattle from before dawn to well after dusk.

Last year it had also become a period of flaring tempers against Sam Hook. Each little half-breed calf trotting beside its Hereford mama was an occasion for rage for ranchers like Ham Bark and Bert Stern. They scarcely saw

114

the calf: what they saw was a ten-dollar loss. And when they saw many hundreds of those ten-dollar losses their tempers burned hotter than the branding irons. This spring, I figgered, the threats against Sam Hook would have to be taken serious.

To make matters worse, almost none of them longhorn cows of Hook's ever dropped a crossbreed. The reason was simple enough. Them longhorn bulls of his, with them six or eight feet of curling horn, were kings of the range. They could gore a short-horned bull, or a polled Hereford bull, slick as an icepick in butter. Some of them Hereford bulls died of it, and others took a mess of doctoring all the time. That just made them ranchers all the hotter against Hook, and threatening to hang the old man from the nearest cottonwood tree. I worried some that them crews, loyal to the brand as always, would take their bosses serious and go do it some day.

This spring things looked worse than ever. That south valley was tensed up and steaming worse than a Yellowstone geyser. The breeding problem was bad enough, but this time all the talk down there was about the hanging of Dale Kratz and about Hook's warning that others would meet the same fate if any more of his bulls were rustled.

Them stockmen, they couldn't stand it. On the one hand they knew Hook was well within his rights. Shooting them bulls was rustling and rustling was a hanging offense in them parts. Most of them had strung up hardcases for a lot less – mavericking some calf, for example. So they knew Hook had a case. And that just drove them crazy because they wanted them bulls of Hooks shot dead, every last one. All that guilt about doing the thing they'd always condemned, and all that anger against Hook, it was too much for them and they were starting to act ringy as a steer full of locoweed. The south end of Meagher County just seethed like a geyser getting ready to shoot off, and there wasn't nothing I could do about it.

Hook must have figgered it too because he suddenly proposed a powwow and said he had an offer, a compromise, in mind. He was wise enough not to send one of his Injuns over to Ham Bark's because that Injun would have been sent home dead, with all them hands remembering Dale Kratz. So Hook sent Jerome Padlock up to me in White Sulphur. The boy said that Hook wanted a meeting with all the stockmen over to Bark's. They usually got together over there about now anyway to plan the roundup, so there was some sense in it. And Bark's was always the gathering place, down there on the south flanks of those craggy Castles, and central to just about everybody.

I could see why Hook wanted that powwow. He and them two bucks had to be at that roundup or the others would steal him blind. Hook figgered he had to make peace and show his face at that roundup, or he'd lose a mess of calves, and maybe worse.

Well, I sent word on down to Bark to set it up for Sunday, and I told him that old Hook was coming in to make some proposition or other. But the thing worried me. There were them that'd just as soon spit a bullet at the old man. Strunck was one. Maybe even Ham Bark. Hook backed him down that day, and that would still rankle a man like Hamilton Bark. And that wasn't the bottom of it neither. That crazy widow would be there too, maybe with that carbine of hers just looking for the right moment. I figgered I'd better attend that powwow myself just to keep the lid on that kettle. I didn't want Hook dying of lead poisoning on me. If the truth be known, I'd gotten so I sort of respected that old codger, although I hated to admit it. The ranchers and their hands are tough customers and I didn't cotton to the idea of bracing them, but maybe I wouldn't have to. Just having the law around was worth something. I'd wear the star and they'd see it plain.

And I'd run a quick search of Widow Thwait's buggy too, just in case she had a notion to bring in that carbine.

I sent word along to Bark that I'd be there and that I didn't want toughs or drovers or hardcases on hand – just the stockmen and maybe their foremen. I figgered they'd ignore that. Them ranchers would all troop in with a handful of their feistiest lads, just to put heat on Hook. But Hook didn't fear up that easy. In the end, it all would depend on that old stubborn man. If he talked sense and said he'd sell off them longhorns, the whole thing would pass over and be done with. But I had a hunch he had something else in mind. Otherwise he would have just sold his stock without no announcements of it.

Sunday morning, under a gray overcast, Tin backed my bay into the traces and buckled up, then I set off for Ham's. I figgered maybe I could put into the county for some sabbath pay and see what them tightwads did with a voucher like that. Probably eat it.

That Smith River country is some of the bleakest land a man can set eyes on, especially on a gray day. I got the bay jogging along pretty good but it wasn't much of a day to be enjoying scenery. The overcast blackened all the ponderosa on the slopes and whitened all the sagebrush in the valley. There's a lot of places where the river drops from view down between mean gray cliffs, and some places so barren you'd give your right arm to see a tree.

The Castles to the east, they were some better, full of spires like a pirate palace on a cliff. But the tops were sliced off by the overcast, like the humptops of the Big Belts, Grassy Mountain, Horse Butte and all. Egghumps pushing into the cloud. Some of the Sixteen Mile country where Hook ranched was bleak too, but not around his home place where the Bridgers humped greenly off to the south.

It wasn't so much cold as it was high-country dull, and I hurried the bay along. I wanted to get to Ham's early and check out a few things as folks arrived, namely who was wearing iron and not unbuckling it around polite folk. At Horse Butte, where I cut east toward Bark's place, I could see black horse-dots off in the distance making toward the powwow.

When I pulled up to Ham Bark's there was Winfrid Coop, politely asking folk to hang up their guns on the pegs along the bunkhouse wall. (I guess Bark figgered that a shooting might tarnish his hospitality a little.) Winfrid wasn't taking no for an answer, neither, and there was a growing collection of iron dangling from them logs.

"Guess I'll keep mine, Win," I said.

He looked at me sharp. "I guess you will, Sheriff," he replied. "Ham didn't like the feel of this so he's got me on a peace mission."

"I figgered it. You ain't gonna get the hideouts and the stickers though."

He grinned. "Now who'd be sporting one of those?"

Ham had set up the conflagration in his yard, and his boys had dragged in a bunch of logs and stumps for sitting. Mrs. Bark had a trestle table on sawhorses loaded down with coffee and the like. I didn't see no spirits, and I figgered maybe Bark was making some sense there, too.

The widow came rattling up in that old trap of hers and she surprised me some, being in brown gingham skirts and all. I was so used to seeing her in bib overalls, or sometimes jeans when she was feeling flouncy, that I reacted to them skirts.

She saw me staring. "When a lady wants a man, she's got to dress up for it," she said cheerily.

That struck me as downright flirtatious for a crazy lady. Maybe she was turning over a leaf.

Soon as I could, I sidled on over to Win Coop.

"She bring any hardware?"

"None I could see."

"Kind of block her view, will you? I want a quick look at that trap of hers."

I slid a hand around under the seat and below the box and floorboards and all. That rig was clean. There was no thirty-thirty carbine slippered in there anywhere. So I let it be. She'd be okay. I could see her flushed up and socializing some with Mrs. Bark, talking like she hadn't done in years.

They were piling in fast now, Stern and Monk and a handful of toughs, including Strunck. That riled me some. I'd sent him out of the county and here he was, bold as could be, like there was no sheriff here and there weren't half a dozen flyers out on him. He unbuckled for Win so cheerful that I figgered he had two irons in his boots and a sticker or two up his sleeves. That would bear watching.

Hook showed up on his roan, rising up from behind a little crest west of Ham's lane. He just stopped there and stared for a moment, missing nothing. Then he walked the roan on down toward the pens. I watched the old man climb down lithe as a kid. He lifted the scattergun from a special saddle sheath he had for it and started toward the picnic.

Win frowned and trotted on over to him.

"Howdy Sam," he said. "Ham's inviting folk

to hang their iron over there to the bunk-house." The way he said it, it wasn't any request.

Hook glanced at the bunkhouse and over at the crowd too, and he seen I was the only one with iron but he didn't relax none. There was the barest pause and then he said, quietlike, "Thanks, Win. I've no belt so I guess I'll just pack this back in my saddle sheath if you don't mind."

He stared at Win Coop in a way that said that Win wouldn't mind. Then he slid that cannon into the sheath.

"Leave him saddled," he directed. "I won't rain on this picnic for more than half an hour and there's no point in uncinching."

"Suit yourself, Sam," said Win.

Hook didn't drift toward the crowd on the lawn. He cocked a knowing eye at me, drifted on over to Widow Thwait's rig, and slipped a hand around and under.

"I already checked," I said to him. "She's wearing nothing but gingham and a few layers of whatever."

The faintest of smiles built up around the crowsfeet of his eyes and he glided off as quiet as a hunting catamount, leaving a wake of silence and hard stares behind him. There sure wasn't nobody busting out of the crowd to howdy him or gladhand the old loon. Unless he had one of them bucks stashed in the bushes, he was as alone as any mortal man gets to be. I could dang near smell the fire and brimstone boiling up in them stockmen as they eyed old Hook. I wasn't going to allow no violence so I just meandered into the bunch, staying close to Hook and my hand not far from my ivory grip.

The stragglers were churning in now and it looked like just about the whole south end of Meagher County was pretty well on hand. There were a lot more hired help than I would have liked, too. Maybe a hundred people in all, with the stockmen over on the lawn and them hands huddling around the bunkhouse and a few kids all over. The stockmen looked dark and silent, but them hands were all lighting up cheroots and swapping big windies.

I ain't never seen a man so alone as Sam Hook. He didn't seem afraid except maybe coiled up some inside so that he seemed to glide instead of walk. I confess, I had to admire him. It took a heap of courage to wander in there with no protection at all except his good reputation, and to stand there like one of them East Indian untouchables, everyone making a wide berth around him like he was a one-man cholera epidemic.

His eyes, they just rested calm on one man after another, sizing up, I'd say, filing away information about mood and spirit and meanness in the face. Not even Ham Bark, usually a pretty decent host, came on over to Hook with a welcome. Ham just stood off there at the edge, uneasily studying the earth, shading from pink to orange to pink again. I hankered to go on over and pass the time of day with Hook but I didn't. If I done that, I'd lose the election for sure. It was Widow Thwait he was studying the most, only he didn't show it — he just seemed to be glancing around. She was working at ignoring him, I could see that.

Ham Bark stood up on a stump and got the show going.

"Sam Hook wants to say a few words," he announced abruptly, "and after that we'll plan the spring roundup."

Hook stepped up on the stump and waited for all them stockmen to quiet down. It didn't take long. He seemed old and frail up there, facing down that wall of hate around him. But somehow it was an even match: Hook on one side weighing as much as all them others together.

"My crew and I have been building four-wire fence around two sections of my land, and we'll be done shortly," he began. "At the spring roundup I'll cut out my broodstock – cows, heifers, bulls – and turn them into that enclosure for sixty days. That's how much grass is in there. And that will cover most of the breeding season."

Nobody said nothing.

"After that," Hook continued in that cracked high voice, "they'll go back out on public range where they have every right to be.

"Now I suggest you purebreed breeders do the same. Control your breeding. As you know, there's ten, twelve drovers here building their own small herds, all with common cattle, as you call the longhorns. They've a right to public range too. And their bulls can breed your purebloods as easy as mine.

"Now let's do it fair and square. If I pull my beeves off public grass for two months, it seems to me you should do so also. That little rest will give the range some growth for fall, too. Nothing but steers on it for two months.

"That's my proposition. It's fair. It's some goodwill from me asking for some goodwill from you. It's costing me plenty, and it'll cost you some too. But it'll solve the problem for us all."

That was it, then. The stiff old man just stood there on the stump waiting. It did sound pretty fair to me, but I knew down in my bowels that it was too late. Them stockmen wouldn't bend an inch.

Bert Stern always fancied himself an orator and he answered for them all. "The answer's no, Hook," he said with sledgehammer words. "You're going to get rid of every damned longhorn now, or the district is going to do it for you."

There was pure stonewall in them words and I could see that was the way of it with all them stockmen.

There was a knowing glint in Hook's eye, and he began a quiet head count.

"Is that your view, Ham?" he asked so softly that it sounded silky and civilized compared to Stern's shouting.

Ham didn't say nothing. Just the faintest nod.

"Dan?" asked Hook.

Monk just glanced elsewhere, damned if he'd say a word.

"Abe?"

Stapp done the same, coughed and stared at the clay.

"Mary Ellen?" he asked so softly it could hardly be heard.

She just laughed sort of hysterical.

Then all the rest, Stone and Jung, neighbors of Hook's down there on the Sixteen, and all.

And they all said nothing, like a bunch of thunderheads across the whole horizon, silent but full of blue flashes.

Hook got to the end of it and sighed.

"I'll see you at the roundup," he murmured, his old voice cracking with his own tension.

"No, you won't," snarled Stern. "You aren't invited and you wouldn't find it healthy." He sort of underlined that last word.

Hook paused, absorbing that. It was out in the open now, the thing they were going to do. Naked and ugly. It didn't take words or explaining. Hook knew and everyone else knew. If Hook and his Injuns showed up at that roundup, they'd be hanged as fast as the others could haul them to a cottonwood. At the least, I figgered, them stockmen would shoot every longhorn bull that got driven in by the drovers, and they'd cut every longhorn bullcalf too. And then they'd burn their brands into the young hides of Hook's entire increase. It was going to be undiluted two hundred-proof theft. They didn't see it that way, of course. They were just going to compensate themselves for all the trouble and loss that Hook had caused them, property be damned.

That sure got me to squirming. What they were getting set to do was illegal as hell and crooked besides. And the law, namely me, was just about helpless to stop it. I seen them stormclouds building now, thunder rolling down the mountains, fire and brimstone piercing down to strike Sam Hook and his ranch and his beeves and his Injuns in one violent storm.

Hook knew it too. He didn't say nothing, just stood there frozen, thinking, sticking up there stiff and tall like a lightning rod.

"I'll see you at the roundup," he repeated softly, and stepped down and walked right through the middle of them toward the corrals. We all just gawked there, rooted to the clay, watching that stiff man glide off toward his twitchy-eared roan. Watching, watching, and hating.

And then, before he got there, it happened.

CHAPTER 10

First I knew, Mary Ellen Thwait was hurtling toward Hook, stumbling inside her brown gingham skirts since she hardly wore that type of clothing any more.

Hurrying toward Hook. And then a pop, no more than a firecracker pop, and I seen she had a lady gun, a little five-shot thirty-two calibre job she'd concealed in them skirts somewhere. And another pop. And another pop just as Hook reached his horse.

And that time she got him. The left side of his head. He was slammed back onto the saddle skirts, clawing at the saddle, losing his senses, starting to slide down.

Then, still going down, he yanked that shotgun from that sheath, and swung around and shot, the crack of it jarring the air. Suddenly Widow Thwait, she didn't have a head, just a mess of red and gray ooze where buckshot caught her point-blank. She hit the earth dead. Hook was down beside the sidestepping roan, senseless, the shotgun lying in manure.

129

I rushed in there, with Winfrid Coop, but most of the rest hung back, afraid of taking lead. I seen Mary Ellen and my guts turned over on me. Hook, I didn't know whether he was dead or just dying. Win Coop knelt down beside him and said, "He's breathing."

We rolled Hook over and I had a quick look at that mess on Hook's head.

"I can't tell for certain with all this blood, but it looks like he was grazed. Plowed a furrow along his skull over the ear," Win said.

And then, as if that wasn't enough, something else happened that still gives me the willies. Jerome Padlock rose right out of the grass, out of nowhere, like a ghost, with a mean six-gun in his hand and some kind of fire blazing in those black eyes. Next I knew he'd backed us all off, Win Coop, myself, and several hands. He whipped out a blue bandanna and tied it tight around the old man's head, and the bandanna turned black with blood. Then as gentle as a sheepherder with a newborn lamb he lifted the old cuss onto the roan. The old man was still unconscious, but out of some deep instinct he wrapped his bony hands around the horn and hung on with a death grip.

Then Jerome backed away slowly with his own pistol holstered and Hook's mean shotgun facing us. He backed clear over the rise, never taking his black eyes off us. Then there was a long silence and the hurry of two distant horses.

Nobody said much. Them as had guts to look at what was left of the widow sort of sidled close and then backed away. Mrs. Bark and one or two other ladies disappeared into the house. It was mortuary quiet around there, with the shock of death under them low clouds. The widow's hands, Len Carroll and Kid Dunham, were around somewheres, and pretty soon I seen them coming from a shed, with some canvas and rope. They stared at her some, gagging a little, and then they stretched the canvas, rolled her into it, and tied up. The pair of them, looking green-faced, picked up the bundle carefully and carried it off to her trap.

Old Dunham, battered sombrero in hand, he said to me, "Guess we'll drive her up to Jethro. I don't know what next."

I didn't know, neither. Dunham harnessed up the rig, tied his own bronc behind, and drove off under a gray sky, with Len Carroll following slow and quiet. Pretty soon they disappeared over the ridge, too.

Bert Stern spat. "He killed a woman and he'll hang for that."

I didn't like the tone of the remark, so I laid

it to rest fast: "That was the clearest case of self-defense I ever heard of." I said it loud enough to carry to all them hands hunkered along the bunkhouse. I looked over thataway, and chilled up. Every one of them six-shooter belts that had been pegged was gone, hanging on its owner. Now there were sixty or seventy fingers a few inches away from sixty or seventy triggers.

The jugs had appeared. Someone had busted into Ham Bark's spirits and uncorked, and now everywhere I glanced I seen a jug or a green bottle uptilted or a tin cup passing along. In ten or fifteen minutes this bunch would take leave of its senses, and God knows what would happen. I began to sweat on my belly.

"You all get along home now," I yelled. "This meeting's over."

Nobody moved.

I stalked over to the great orator, Bert Stern. "Here, now, Bert. You get your crew together and ride on home. That's the sensible thing in a time of trouble."

Stern just laughed. "Get lost, fat boy," he said.

I buttonholed Ham. "Better break this up and get them bozos off your place, Ham. There's been enough grief in your yard for a lifetime, and I don't like the way this is going."

"The hell with that," he retorted. "After what we all just saw, womankilling and all, a little corn spirits is what a man needs bad to get steadied down. Maybe it'll get us fixed to hang that old murderer after a while."

"You're not going to do that," I said. "There'll be a proper inquest with witnesses, and the law will decide. This is going to be done right."

He leered. "You going to stop us, Oglesby?"

"I'll do my level best," I replied. "That was pure self-defense and you and every man knows it. You'd have done the same."

"I don't care what it was. He's going to hang. Been asking for a noose a long time. If the law doesn't do it in about ten minutes, we will."

I turned away, disgusted. And plain worried. Them thunderclouds hadn't gone away; they'd turned into towering granddaddy thunderheads with anvil tops clean across the horizon. I needed help.

I found Win Coop out at the pens. He was as tough and level as any man I knew. He was Ham's loyal foreman, but maybe . . .

"Win, there's hell brewing."

He nodded.

"Are you Ham's foreman pure and total, or are you a man with your own mind and all . . ."

He stared at me quizzical.

"I don't want a lynching and that's the way this is twisting. They're liquoring up to hang Sam Hook. I need someone to beat it to town fast and get —"

"I know what you want; saw the question in your face before you said it. Sure, I'll do it. Probably too late, though. Helluva long way. Two hours on a fast horse to White Sulphur, a half hour to line up a few sobersides, and then five hours of hard riding to Hook's spread." He shook his head. "I'll do it, though. I've a young stud in there with bottom. It'll be a good run for him."

I felt some small relief as I watched him saddle and light out.

"Where the hell's he going?" Ham demanded.

"Keeping an eye out for your interests," I replied.

Bark laughed. "He's too late."

It hit me cold as March rain that they were gonna do it. Self-defense or not, that didn't matter. Shooting Widow Thwait, womankilling, that didn't matter to them. That was just the excuse for what they'd been itching and panting to do for two years now. I could argue the logic of self-defense until I was purplefaced and it wouldn't nudge them. I could argue law, and inquests, and witnesses and evidence and proper procedure, and they wouldn't listen. They were building toward the crazies, and logic or reason or order or law was all nothing. They were crawling down into their animal selves, and I was standing there watching them do it.

A chill came over me as I realized they were fixing to hang Hook because he didn't go along with the bunch. He had always been the maverick, the loner, going his own way, heeding his own counsel. He was the outsider, the lone bull that the herd couldn't stand, and now they'd gore him and pull him down. Maybe it was because Hook didn't really need them, didn't even need the grazing district. He got along fine with just himself and two Blackfeet Injuns, asking nothing.

It hit me like ice crystals in my windpipe that it was all up to me. Me wearing that tin star was the only thing between that mob and that old man's life. And I didn't have no magic to stop them. That tin star, what was it? Just a hunk of potmetal – unless there was a man behind it that could turn it into brass or steel or gold or silver. That danged star began to weigh me down like a lead sinker on my chest. I was always a pretty good politician, and that kept me in office, but now this here job was asking me to be something more than a baby-kisser, and I didn't know how.

I figgered maybe to cut off the booze that bunch was drinking, and to do it fast, so I pulled my six-gun and swung it butt-first into a jug and that jug shattered. Then I knocked three, four green bottles all to bits.

"What the hell you doing, Oglesby?" yelled someone, and all them with bottles and jugs ran off and hid the stuff.

"Get the hell back to White Sulphur where you belong," some kid yelled.

"Get along home now," I yelled back. "We're going to stay peaceful around here."

They laughed. The whole mob of them howled like coyotes.

The stockmen were hunkered down around the front yard and the drovers and hands were on over to the bunkhouse and corrals, and I figgered to talk turkey to the stockmen because they were the levelheaded ones, and the ones to give orders. They weren't saying much, just passing the jugs and looking tickled at what was to come. I simply sat down with them and took a belt when the jug passed by. Then I started in, quiet and calm.

"Hook's a loner," I said soft, "always liked to do things his own way. A strong man, too. I guess them trapping years did that, all alone up there in them mountains year after year. It pulled him apart from the run of us."

"He's a pain in the butt's what he is," said Bark.

"Good strong place he has there," I said. "Heavy shutters and loopholes. He could hold off an army and hurt a lot of folk. Them three in there, bulletproof, firing out at anything that moves. It'd take a week to bust into that."

"Nothing a little fire can't fix," said Abe Stapp.

"I don't think so," I said. "Copper roof on that house and sod on the barns."

No one said much for a bit.

"He's more a man than the bunch of us put together," I said, very quiet.

"Oglesby, you get out of here. This isn't your business," bellowed Dan Monk.

"The law's staying and keeping the peace," I said. "Long as I wear this star, nobody's stringing up anyone. Least of all Sam Hook," I said. "If need be, I'll get into that house and make it four, one on each side, defending it."

I sort of surprised myself, saying that. There was no answer from anyone.

"The thing you can't stand is that he runs his spread according to his own notions. You've been butting in on his life and his ways, and he's ignored you, and now you're fixing to hang him for being different."

Bert Stern's face turned ugly and next I knew he had his big Smith and Wesson pressed into my belly. "One more word from you and this goes off. Each word you say, my trigger finger twitches."

I was sweating bad now. He was liquored up and I was scared he might just do it, law and star and sheriff or not. I could feel my guts lurching around in there.

I was scared so bad I almost yelled, but I just backed off, little mincing steps backward. I didn't care how it looked to them. If I got tough or talked sheriff-talk, I was a dead man. They were all grinning and swigging and chortling as I got twenty, thirty, forty feet back. I was so scared that all I wanted to do was point my horse north and wheel on out of there. But I was in deep now and feeling the weight of that star. Potmetal star, potmetal sheriff, I thought, hating my cowardice and the whole miserable mess. Hating Hook, too, for causing it.

I forced my boots to toe toward that other bunch, the drovers, so's to work on them a little, and not liking it because some of them were hardcases and they were all full of sour-mash now.

I didn't even get close. Strunck seen me and whipped a shot at me that snarled an inch from my ear. I froze stiff as he snickered. "Next one's

138

headed for between your eyes, fatso. Don't come to us with your preaching. In a few minutes Hook's going to be dead, just as dead as my old friend Dale Kratz."

I stood there alone, just as alone as Sam Hook ever was. Soon enough the whole pack ignored me, and got back to its liquoring. Fifteen, twenty stockmen and twenty, thirty drovers, in two murderous bunches, starting to spill out animal smell, wolf noise. It was a bad thing.

I stood at the corrals, not part of any of it. I figgered Win Coop was about to town by then. But he'd never make it in time. This whole thing was heading up and boiling over too fast. This outfit was minutes away from mounting up and riding off to a lynching. I seen one of those bozos building nooses with his lariat.

I got me a notion that might slow the party down some. Not for long, though. I eased slow and careful into the corrals and looked around. It was about the way I figgered — lots of saddles and bridles hanging on the corral poles, and a few broncs saddled and bridled. I fussed a little around my buggy, as if I was fixing to light out, and slipped out my jackknife. The blade was dull, but it would do. I sort of meandered through the saddled horses first, as if chasing my bay, but on the far side of each I began cutting reins and letting the ends slip into the manure. There was one nice Mex braided rawhide outfit, and I let that one be. I went back and fiddled with my buggy a little, and backed the bay in and buckled him. Then I eased over to all them bridles draped along the corral poles, and began slicing along there, too. I was plenty scared there'd be some whoop and holler and hot lead coming. But none did. They had their vision set on nooses now, and they weren't playing all that close attention to an overweight sheriff.

Pretty soon I had all the reins cut and mixed up in manure, except for three, four bridles that were over near the bunkhouse and close to that mob of drovers. I just had to let them be.

I figgered maybe to work on the cinches next. The reins they could splice in a few minutes. A little baling wire twisted around the butt ends would make a good temporary splice. I done it many times out on the road and so had most of them buckaroos. Half of them didn't need reins anyway. They all had rawhides thong in their kits and they'd just tie that on and it'd work fine. But cinches, that was another matter entirely. Cut them strands and it meant a trip to town for a new one, or a long time repairing and patching. But I never had a chance.

Strunck, he rose up like a red-headed demon and howled.

"Let's go get him," he roared. They were all ready. And that did it. One by one they stood up and stretched and headed for the corral.

Me, I lit out in my buggy, thanking all the powers of the universe I had got my bay hooked up beforehand. I was pretty well down the lane and out to the road when I heard an angry howl back there, like a mess of enraged bears. There was some popping and banging but I was way beyond six-gun range. I whipped that bay into a fast trot, the kind that ate miles, and figgered I had a good half hour on them before they got repaired and mounted. Especially in their liquored-up condition.

I turned west, got sight of Horse Butte, and set the bay toward the Sixteen country and Sam Hook's. I didn't want to go, but that star was saying I had to.

CHAPTER 11

It was a quiet ride. Montana's a quiet place. I bored along westward hearing nothing but the hoofbeats of the bay, the grind of the buggy wheels, and the creak of leather.

There was no one behind me. I must have snarled them up pretty good. In my possibles box was a small spyglass — a handy tool for sheriffing — and I scanned my back trail now and then. There wasn't nothing back there.

I figgered they'd be along, though. They were coming, no doubt about it. A small army of them, liquored up, with a hanging on their minds. I didn't figger they'd bother me in spite of the cut reins. They'd written me off long ago, much as I hate to admit it. Hook was someone to contend with, but not Will Oglesby.

I headed down into the sagebrush bottoms of the south fork of the Smith, which I had to cross to get to Hook's Sixteen Mile country. That worried me some. There was a good ford there, a wide slab of rock that stream ran over before cascading into small rapids. It was May, and the mountain runoff was at its peak.

I pulled up at the stream bank and clambered out for a close look. It was bad. The stream was roiling and high and murky, two or three feet above what I knew was safe. I thought some of just tacking north on up to White Sulphur. Hook could take care of himself, especially with that bastion of a house and help coming from Winfrid Coop in a few hours. Maybe. I didn't need to risk the bay, the buggy, and myself getting swept into those rapids.

I sighed. I sure don't know what was itching at me then, but I got back into my rig and reined that bay down to the edge. He wasn't none too happy. I lifted my shiny black buggy whip from its socket and gave that bay a real crack over the croup. He plowed forward, with water soon up to his belly. Near the far shore I could feel the current tugging at those wheels and threatening to upend that horse, too. The buggy kept sliding sideways with the pressure. Water boiled up over the floorboards and I got my boots up out of it. There was a bad moment when the rig careened off on two wheels, and then came down slow, but by then the bay was hauling up the far bank and we gushed on out of there, sloshing water. I stopped and let the big bay shake and spray, and I caught a mess of muddy icewater all over my good suit and the black enamel of the buggy.

Still no sign of nobody behind and that felt good. But I was running down in the bottoms now and didn't have much horizon. I sensed time was running out. I had to get licking before that mob boiled up and ran past me. I cussed myself for racing to that old man. He didn't need me and he'd never treated me as much of anything.

I snapped that bay into a fine trot and let him run. Hook was right. That animal was a looker but he didn't have much bottom, so I alternated walks and trots.

At the Sixteen Mile turnoff I stopped for a look around. Nothing. That trip through the choked up Sixteen country began to unnerve me because I couldn't see any horizon — just a long funnel of relentless duty with no side roads all the way to Hook's spread.

When I finally did pull in there, an hour later, it was all so quiet and peaceful you'd never imagine a mob was fixing to come here and hang someone. One thing struck me right off — a rig parked off to one side, a two-horse phaeton that looked some familiar but I couldn't rightly place it. And there was a pair of dappled grays harnessed, flicking off a few spring flies. I'd seen the outfit somewhere.

I thought maybe Hook was dead and this was some outfit of Jethro's, but it wasn't. Could be Doc Easum's, I figgered. Only that didn't make no sense, Doc waiting here, six, seven hours from White Sulphur, to treat an injury that happened maybe four hours ago.

That phantom Jerome upped from somewhere and I told him to run my buggy into the corral. When I reached the house Padlock opened the door. Behind him stood Hook, gray as the overcast skies, looking sick as he peered through two black eyes, real shiners. He had a new white bandage, though. Inside was dark: all them heavy bullet-stopping shutters had been drawn shut and bolted, and the inside was pure gloom.

"What's your business, Oglesby?" Hook rasped. He sure looked sick.

"They're coming. They're getting all liquored up for a noose party. I tried to stop them, and did slow that whole caboodle down by cutting all their reins. But they're coming for you, Hook and I ain't been able to stop it. They're plumb crazy and working themselves up, and I don't intend to have any necktie parties in my county."

He looked at me and smiled faintly. "Thank you, Sheriff. Good of you. Come in, you're just in time for some festivities."

When I stepped through the dark hallway and into the big room, which was lit by a lazy fire in the long fireplace, danged it I didn't get a jolt. There was Maud Wall, of all people, all dolled up in a silvery blue silk affair with a hundred little buttons up her female front, and a mess of daisies in her hand. And the sot, Francis Harp, gaunt and raven-haired and dressed like a penguin. And then I seen that Hook was in city clothes. I'd never seen him in a suit before, celluloid collar, and white cuffs peering out from sleeves. Handsome devil, lean and manly, even sick like that. He looked bad, though, ashen and shaking. And over to the long fireplace was the owner of that rig, that Methodist preacher at White Sulphur, Ormly Richard, and him in a black robe with a white stole dangling around his scrawny neck, and a Testament in hand.

"Sheriff, you've met everyone?" Hook asked calmly. "Come then, and share our moment of joy with us."

I nodded, still absorbing it all. "How's your head?" I blurted.

"Terrible. It throbs and pounds and nauseates. It's better when I'm resting with my eyes closed."

"But why this, now . . . ?"

"This celebration was to have been this evening, but under the circumstances we moved it ahead. Fortunately, everyone had arrived this morning. But now – it would be well for the Reverend Mr. Richard to be off and gone. Before the troubles. And the rest."

Padlock, I noticed, stalked from loophole to loophole in the shuttered gloom. Jerome was no doubt off scouting.

Maud Wall was a sight. Waves of feeling transfixed her face, one way and then another; fear following anger, and love and tenderness all mixed in with the rest.

"Let's be on with it. Time is of the essence," intoned Francis Harp. "Mr. Oglesby, this is most fortuitous. We shall have you witness the document, if you will."

I had a skullful of questions – why now? What started this? Where would they live? When were them drunks coming, and what then? But I just stood aside, antsy and itchy, while Ormly Richard cleared his throat. The man had a voice ten mountain ranges lower than a bull, and he rumbled into the business like a trumpeting moose.

"Dearly beloved," he thundered, "we are gathered together before God to join in holy matrimony Samuel Hook and Maud Wall . . ."

I remembered to pull off my Four-X beaver

hat, and I just stood there fingering it and thinking this was the craziest thing I ever did see, a hang-noose honeymoon. I had a wild itch to peer through them loopholes myself but I didn't. I just kept my eye on Hook, who looked about ready to keel over and was leaning heavy into Maud's arm.

I began to think maybe this was Harp's doing, a lawyer's way of getting this ranch anchored down the way Hook wanted. But dammit, this here was no marriage of convenience. Them two were lovebirds, I could see that plain. That look on Maud's face, which made her beauteous and tender-glowing, that look told me all I figgered I needed to know. If Harp had a hand in it, it was only to rush along what was coming anyway. Hook, he was too sick to have any expression except pure pain.

Reverend Richard had got us through the preliminaries and a prayer, and was getting down to the business end of the ceremony, pledges and rings and all, when Jerome slid in and interrupted.

"They're a mile off," he said flatly. "Maybe fifty in all." He barred the door behind him and picked up a carbine. I thought I heard the howling hooves right then, but it was just my jittery imagination in that quiet room.

Richard looked sharp at the Injun, flipped

past a couple of pages, and got right into the red meat of it.

"Samuel, will you take Maud to be your lawful wedded wife, to have and to hold, for better or worse, in sickness and in health, for as long as you shall live?"

"I will," said Sam Hook.

Then it was Maud's turn and soon enough her "I will" was said, strong and sweet as sagebrush scent in rain.

I could hear them locoes out there clear now, bloodthirsty yells as that wolfpack thundered off the Sixteen Mile road and on up the ranch lane. It was a fearsome sound that shrunk me up inside.

"Therefore," Richard thundered with a voice rolling down the mountains, "by the authority vested in me as an ordained minister of Christ, I pronounce you man and wife. What God hath joined together, let no man put asunder."

Maud and Hook collapsed into each other's arms, and I seen the shiny gold band on her finger. The two just hung there clinging, and Harp looked pleased, and Richard fussed with his gear.

Then Harp was thrusting some parchment at Richard, and they went over to Hook's big desk and began dipping the nib into the inkwell and scratching on that sheet. I took the pen and got my fingers stained, found the witness line and, careful as I could, considering how my hand shook, I wrote in Wilbur Oglesby, and it was done and witnessed. Harp blotted and then snatched it up and into his breastpocket.

What next? I wondered. *What next?*

As if in answer, Padlock fired, and the clap of it shattered the peace. Acrid powder smoke boiled into the room. I sure didn't know what he fired at but the mob out there grew powerful silent. I raced over to a loophole for a peep, and I seen them off a ways, standing careful and far enough away to make poor targets, although there were bunches spreading to the flanks to surround the place. Some others had spotted the buggies and looked to be arguing about them. They recognized mine, but not the other, I figgered.

Hook was too full of pain and wedlock to be thinking and I knew I had to get him started.

"Sam," I said, "I sent Winfrid Coop up to White Sulphur for help. He lit out fast to get Jethro and some of them up there who are steady. But if they come, that's still three, four hours from now."

"If anyone comes," said Hook, and danged if he wasn't grinning at me. The truth is, I doubted anyone would come down here to tangle with some of the meanest stockmen

150

and hardcases in the county.

He eyed Maud tenderly. "We'll get you and the preacher and Francis out of here now. And Oglesby, too. It's too dangerous for any of you to stay. There'll be a siege until they sober up and go home."

Maud's eyes were wet-rimmed, but she looked as strong as United States Steel preferred stock.

"No. Your fate is my fate."

"But Maud —"

Sam wasn't getting anywhere. I figgered he had just lost his first domestic argument. With a wife like that Maud, he was gonna lose more often than win.

"Reverend? We'll get you out. . . . It was uncommonly good of you to come —"

Ormly Richard shook his head. "I have a mind to address them," he rumbled. "There's a few commandments to discuss." He smiled.

Jerome fired again at some unknown target and I heard a horse screech and cough, then thump into the earth, dead or dying. The clap of it battered our ears and more smoke drifted blue through the room. There was a string of cussing out there, then six-guns popping and lead thumping into those log walls, making us all wince.

"Reverend, if you step out that door you'll be

151

cut down," argued Hook.

"Maybe God has brought me to this point of living to be cut down. Cut down like the grasses of summer to make good hay," rumbled the preacher, an octave lower than ever.

On Hook's pain-wracked face I saw respect. A man seeing a man, I thought, a little envious.

The preacher turned his back to us and stalked over to Hook's desk where he sat down, head bowed. I hoped he was saying words for us all.

Then from the outside, a muffled voice called out, "Hook!"

It was the orator, Bert Stern. I peeked out of a loophole and seen him there on his horse, a few yards in front of the others. Somehow it had got to be late afternoon and the gray skies were just graying darker.

"Hook! You're surrounded. You come out of there, you and them two bucks. If you don't, we'll burn you out. You and Oglesby and whoever else you got in there. You come out or they all fry. Even seen a man fry, Hook?"

Hook nodded to Jerome, who fired again, and I seen Stern's big gray gelding go red in the neck and rear up before crumpling to the ground, spilling Stern. Bert Stern sprang up wild as hell, shouting shameful oaths, and then he emptied his six-gun at that loophole —

emptied it, kept pulling the trigger, and finally threw that iron at the house. The thing hit the dinner bell and it gonged. But Jerome had already pegged that loophole and was at another. The slugs slapped blackly into the thick planks, making us all dive sideways. I wasn't sure how sturdy them old shutters were.

Hook sighted and for once in his life seemed indecisive.

"Oglesby," Stern yelled. "You got no business in there. You get out, and anyone else doesn't belong, or you'll fry too. Your tin star isn't going to help you at all."

My gut flipped over but I stepped to a hole and said as soft as I could, so they had to strain to hear, "Go on home, Bert. No one's hanging today. I'm here to arrest the first person who starts trouble."

All that did was loose a bunch of catcalls and jeers, plus a few more six-gun shots into the logs.

Harp found a carbine and stationed himself at a port on the rear side, cool as a seasoned hardcase. Padlock padded back and forth checking two sides.

"Three or four out there with jugs of kerosene, I think," he informed Hook.

Hook turned to me. "Sheriff, I can't yell. My head pounds too much. Tell them that anyone who throws kerosene is a dead man."

"Don't you think we should get along with these folks, Sam, and try to talk a little instead of riling them up any —"

"Tell them."

"This is Sheriff Oglesby," I yelled. "Anyone who throws kerosene toward this house will be shot."

I peeked out and seen three or four of the buckaroos set down jugs fast — whether of kerosene or spirits, I didn't know. I began thinking maybe we'd win this business after all.

"I'll step outside," Maud said. "When they see a woman here, they —"

"No. Those men are liquored up, Maud. Likely as not to shoot anyone who steps out that door."

"I'll do it anyway, Sam. The reason they're here is because of Mary Ellen Thwait . . . what happened. If they feel that strongly about — about killing a woman, then they won't —"

I interrupted. "They didn't care none about Widow Thwait. That was just the excuse. For a long time, they've been looking for a reason to come after Sam here."

She absorbed that quietly.

"Sheriff's right," pronounced Hook.

Her face lifted up. "I intend to make this the most beautiful day of my life. If that means facing them to end this, then I shall face them. If it means dying, then I will die the wife of God's finest man, Sam Hook."

She clenched herself to the old rancher and seemed to pour her own vitality into him. For a long moment there, the pain left his face and was replaced by a tenderness I never imagined was in Sam Hook.

The moment was shattered by a crack, crack, and then a third crack from Padlock's repeater; howls of pain, and a hail of lead from six-shooters. Then quiet. I thought I began to smell kerosene.

"I shot two," Padlock said. "There's a puddle of spilled kerosene out a rod or so from the wall."

"Are they dead?" asked Hook.

"No. Leg and arm. Bleeding hard. Being hauled back."

"Good."

From my loophole I saw a bunch of them rush to the barn and began to tug at an old wagon. Some started to pile logs and silvery old planks on it. Others got pitchforks and began to pile hay on it.

"They're making a fire wagon," I told Sam. "Shielded too. From these high holes we'll hardly even get a shot at their feet."

He sighed, looking more uncertain than ever.

He was a different Sam Hook from the one I'd always known.

"It's your last chance, Hook. You come out or everyone in there fries to death."

A ragged cheering and hooting followed Stern's new threat, and there was an animal keening in that sound that gave me shivers.

Ormly Richard arose from his prayers.

"I will address them, now. They will hear the Word."

"No —"

But there was no one to stay him. With nothing but a Testament in hand, he unbolted the door and stepped out.

CHAPTER 12

I grabbed a hunting rifle from Hook's gunrack and some shells, and stuck it through one of them loopholes covering the verandah. I figgered if some drunken cowboy shot at the reverend, or was about to, I'd blow that bastard out of his saddle.

But no one shot.

Mr. Richard stood there on that high porch looking 'em over.

"Whoever you are, get out of there," bawled Stern. "Throw up your hands and walk toward us."

"I'm the Reverend Ormly Richard," he boomed. "Some of you know me. I've married some of you. Baptized your children. And buried your dead."

"Cut the speech, preacher. And get out fast or you'll get in the way of some flying lead."

"I will say what I have to say."

"I'm counting to ten. If you ain't over here by then, we'll put you off there. One, two, three . . ."

157

"I'll shoot anyone touches him," I yelled.

Stern snarled, "You're on the wrong side, Oglesby, and you'll fry in there. Four, five, six . . ."

Mr. Richard smiled. "I will come down among you and we will talk further." He walked down the verandah steps.

"Seven, eight . . ."

I seen some flap-eared jasper fixing to lasso the reverend, so I drew a careful bead on his hand as he was building a loop, and squeezed. He howled, and that hand, what was left of it, burst red. The crack of that high-powered rifle sure startled that bunch. That jasper waved that arm and sprayed blood over himself, and I seen two fingers missing.

"Oglesby, for that you're going to hang with the rest," someone yelled.

"You'd better take my star off first," I muttered soft.

Mr. Richard stood still. The smile was gone. Then before I could figger what next, two, three loops sailed out and caught him, and he toppled to the grass like a roped dogie. What they done was head-and-heeled him and then they dragged the preacher across the turf like a calf to be branded.

Mr. Richard, all muddied up now, just let them finish, and he stayed calm and unhurt as they trussed him up with his hands tied behind.

He stared up at Stern and Bark and Monk and them others and said, so quiet I could hardly hear through my loophole, "I just stepped out to invite you to a celebration. A party. A blessed event."

That pretty well got their attention.

The reverend sat up. "It was my pleasure this afternoon to marry Sam Hook and Maud Wall. A most joyous event. They are inside preparing a wedding dinner and a joyous honeymoon. We'd like to invite you to the feast."

It sure was quiet out there after that.

"I wish to suggest," he boomed, "that you gents cease your quarrel, lay down your arms, and celebrate this union with us. In God's name."

More silence.

"A wedding celebration is life everlasting. A quarrel is death everlasting, not only of our mortal bodies, but of our souls."

Mr. Richard had said his piece, and sat silent.

I could dang near *see* Hamilton Bark thinking. Maud Wall, Maud Hook with a widow's claim. Hook's ranch and livestock slipping away, just when Bark figgered he could divvy it up with them others and maybe Clay Cott.

Wealth sifting through his fingers like sand. Springs and tanks and patent land and fences. I seen Bark figgering and going orange, his blood up, going hot. And I seen trouble.

But his words weren't hot; they were ice-cold: "Too bad for the woman. She walked into a noose too."

Damn! That sent a chill through me so bad I could hardly stand it. Hang that woman? Stretch her neck from a tree, her in that silvery blue wedding dress? I glanced back at Maud who was sitting near the fire. She'd heard it and had gone ashen. She looked almost as sick as Hook.

"Make another noose," someone out there howled, and there was savage laughter. "We'll hang us a woman; hemp for a lady."

"We're going to have us a honeymoon hanging. A new way to start a marriage."

"Better than the other way," retorted some buckaroo.

I was looking for Strunck, thinking maybe to wing him, but he must have figgered it and hung back in the crowd.

Bark was grinning wolfish and then I seen why. Some buckaroo was lowering a big hemp noose over the preacher's head and drawing it up around his neck.

"Hook! Hook!" yelled Bark. "We're gonna

hang this preacher unless you and those bucks and Maud Wall come on out, right away, single file, hands up. We'll hang the preacher, Hook."

That done it for Maud. I seen tears well up in them honeymoon eyes. She was a brave woman but this was more than she could stand. Hook hugged her and I could see him working ideas around.

He eyed me. "I can't shout. It makes my head split open. You tell them, Sheriff, that we're staying in and that we'll shoot anyone who harms Ormly Richard."

That sounded like the old Hook, but it was too late.

"They've got a noose over him," I said, "and they've dragged him back behind the fire wagon they've made. There's nothing we can shoot at."

"Yes, there is. The stockmen. Bark and Stern and Monk, the ringleaders. But I'm not ready for that. Not yet," he said.

"Make a show of it," suggested Francis Harp. "Let some lead sing, the way a judge's gavel sings."

Hook summoned up a grin. "Good counsel, Counselor. But not to kill. I don't want to see a death here. Not one death on my wedding day. Shoot horses. It's time they began paying a price."

There were broncs aplenty, and I drew a bead on a pretty paint I knew was that kid Ray's pride and joy. He even had a silver-mounted bridle on it.

I squeezed and that paint collapsed with a blue hole betwixt its eyes. The blast in that room was fearsome, and then the noise rang worse, with me and them bucks and Harp all firing. There were shrieks and whinnies and a lot of good horseflesh piling up, and I could see them buckaroos wheeling for cover, some behind the dying animals.

"Enough," rasped Hook. "My head's coming off. Let's save those shells now."

It sure was quiet again, except for the sobs of that kid Ray, who'd taken a bullet in his teen-aged butt out there. I got to thinking we might just make it. We . . . how come I was thinking *we?* I had no more use for that stubborn old man than them ranchers did, but now it was *we* because I was dumb enough to be here, instead of out there. Damn, I hated that star on my vest.

Off beyond the barn and down to the edge of them cottonwoods bordering the Sixteen Mile was the hanging tree. I seen they had four white nooses hanging from a fat cottonwood limb, one for each owner of the Fishhook Ranch. Dangling there in the twilight like some devil's altar.

"Where's the preacher?" Hook asked.

There was something in Hook's voice. The old man seemed to be taking command. He still looked sure-as-hell sick, but his voice was coming strong.

"Behind the wagon, but they're rolling the wagon now — toward the hanging tree."

"Tree? Where? My eyes are no good. Blurred since the concussion."

"Down beyond the barn, toward the river. There's four mean white nooses there, Sam."

Maud looked ghastly pale.

"Four nooses," muttered Hook, pacing back and forth. "How long ago did Win reach town?"

I shook my head. "Sam, don't count on it. I don't figger even Jethro'll come."

He nodded.

Padlock said, "Make a break for it? They're all heading toward the trees."

"Not all," said Jerome.

"They'd hang the reverend," said Sam Hook, "and then us."

Harp weighed in. "A digression? A diversion? Some little entertainment of our own?"

Hook sighed and sat down for a moment beside Maud. "Your hands are icy," he said.

"Warm them for me."

She smiled.

"It's getting dark. We need daylight," he muttered.

I hadn't thought of that. Our rifles and loopholes would be danged near useless under a black overcast sky. Maybe them Injuns could see in the dark but I couldn't and probably not Harp neither. They would soak a couple of walls with kerosene. . . .

"We can make a break on a black night," pressed Harp. "We can create a diversion, and then out the window."

"Into bullets," Hook said, closing the debate.

The wagon was down there at the tree now, mysteriously moving itself. A fifth noose had been thrown over the limb.

"They're gonna hang the preacher now," I said.

Hook sighed. "I'll go out and stop it. Where's my Greener?"

"Sam! No —" Maud cried.

"Don't do it, Hook," I said. "None of us in here can help what's happening. You know they're baiting us with one life in order to take four more."

"One sanctified life, worth ten of mine," he replied. "I can help what's happening. They're cowards, leaning on each other, goading each

164

other to violence, doing things lockstep. Let a man stand firm, use a strong word, and they will break up, flee. I will stand against them."

He found his sawed-off shotgun, slid a shell into the one empty barrel, and checked the other. Each click of it sounded like cannon shot. He dropped a few more shells into his pants pockets.

"Sam! Sam! Oh God, Sam!"

He hugged her. "We're going to have the nicest dinner and honeymoon," he said.

"Sam, oh God, I love you, Sam. Don't go. Please don't."

The crazy old man. I decided to put a stop to this. I trotted over to the door and blocked it.

Sam pried himself from Maud, gentle as possible, and tucked the cold black Greener under an arm.

"Watch for Strunck," he said to Padlock. "And Stern. Bark's got a temper but Stern's the one to go over the edge. Use the old Sharps and the hunting rifle. The range is too far for your carbines."

The Blackfeet padded over to the old man and braced him, two bronze hands on Hook's shoulders. "Sam, don't," he said.

Sam just shook his head and glided toward me.

"You're not going out," I said.

His answer was that shotgun in my gut and a look in his eye that brooked no nonsense from me.

"I'll go with you," I announced.

"No, you won't. One-man job."

"The Sheriff and I will accompany you," said Francis Harp. "These gentlemen will guard Mrs. Hook. Just a minute here, while I find some paper and a pencil."

I glared at that hollow-cheeked sot. A lawyer scrounging paper to take on a deadly mission.

Hook shrugged. "I can't stop you. Stay back and out of my way. I should thank you but I won't because you will make me vulnerable."

So that was the way of it. Cautiously, we opened up that door in the dusk and slid out onto the verandah, two men dressed for a banquet, and a sheriff dressed like a mortician. The mob was busy around that wagon, fixing to string up that preacher and paying no attention to us.

Mr. Richard was going to die brave. I heard that rumbling voice roll up the slope, saying, "My hope is upon paradise. May God forgive you for the wrong you do." That voice rumbled down the valley, and I plumb respected that man.

Hook glided in front of us. There he was, the one that mob lusted for, in string tie, celluloid collar, swallowtail coat, and shiny black patent leather shoes, looking like a dandy at a ball, except for the white bandage binding his head. He sprang farther ahead, twenty, thirty yards ahead, and I marveled that the sickness had fallen away from him like an old husk.

Then them buckaroos got sight of him, and us, and my stomach flipped over and I wished I had a shotgun of my own instead of a miserable six-gun. If you want to control a crowd, use a shotgun. Every sheriff in the country knows that. And damn that Harp, plodding along with a fistful of paper and a pencil, practicing looking stern. Was he going to lecture on Blackstone or something? All I had was a tin star and a six-gun in my sweaty hand. And I hated dying.

We marched on around the wagon, into the leering bunch. And Hook, his Greener square on Stern, said, "Let him go."

Ormly Richard, his face an awful sight, gaped at us.

Stern just giggled. "Got you now, Sam. You're first, and maybe we'll string up Maud next —"

"Let him go," repeated Hook.

"Some honeymoon, eh, boys? Sam and Maud reaching paradise."

Hook's shotgun boomed. What was left of

Bert Stern slid off the saddle and landed in a pulpy red heap.

Two lassos sailed over Hook and were yanked tight. His shotgun went flying. Hook landed on his back, and rolled as ropes yanked him hard. The bunch of them whooped and howled and were down on him in a split second, tying up his feet and lashing his hands behind him.

I was looking for a shot, an opportunity in that melee, but I seen the black bore of Dan Monk's pistol aimed down my throat, and him grinning and giggling, so I lowered mine and stood quiet, puke-sick.

I glanced around, wanting help. Ham Bark was hunkered in his saddle, swigging from a jug and chortling, and hawking up spit gobs at Hook.

"This evens it up now," he yowled. "Evens it all up."

They lifted Hook, frail and light as a down pillow, onto a white bronc and sat him in the saddle sideways because his legs were lashed together. Then they led that white mustang, the kind the Injuns called a medicine horse because of its color, down to the hanging limb.

"I'll arrest every damned one of you," I roared. "Stop this now."

Dan Monk grinned and pulled the hammer back to full cock. But by then I didn't much care. Them others, they just hooted and yowled like Satan himself was in them.

"Have a swig, boys," said Ham, extending the bottle.

Then at last I seen Lorenzo Strunck, that carrot-head glowing even in the dusk, up there slipping a noose over Hook's head and tugging it tight with the knot just behind Hook's left ear. Strunck, he was grinning at me, and I wanted bad to lift that six-gun but I didn't dare, with Monk's black bore down on me. Sam Hook's bandage turned red, new blood oozing through.

Then it got powerful silent. I seen the moon rising and some fog rolling over the cold slopes.

It was Strunck what gave that white horse a lick. It bolted ahead, and Sam Hook was dragged off. The old gent fell; the rope popped and twanged. Hook hit bottom and his neck broke. But he was too light, too frail, and he didn't die right away. He hanged there, twisting, gulping and purpling and rasping, his lips working. And I swear he seen me; them bulging eyes seen me and he rasped out, "Love Maud." Then he died — sagged, swinging quiet, like a pendulum.

Love Maud, *the mother of mothers.*

That stirred some memory, some echo, but I couldn't place it. I cried. No use holding back.

I blubbered. I sat down on the stone and blubbered. No one said nothing, the sickness and stink of it all over that hollow. Sickness and stink everywhere. I heard puking.

It was as quiet as hell. Hook swung there in his string tie and celluloid collar and black swallowtail coat and patent leather shoes.

Lorenzo Strunck wolf-howled, head laid back, rabid into the moon, shivering the hills. "Now let's get the rest," he yowled. "Hows about that there sheriff?"

"Let the others go," rumbled Mr. Richard, like a voice in the burning bush.

"I'm taking names," thundered Francis Harp, and he done the strangest thing. Whacky is the word for it. He whipped out that paper and the stubby pencil and began to glare furiously at one buckaroo after another, scribbling, scribbling.

"He's taking names!" some drover howled. "He's taking down names."

I seen Dan Monk raise his pistol and just before he shot I jammed into his bronc's withers and that shot cracked a little wild, clipping some wool off Harp's black coat.

"I'm taking names," roared Francis Harp. "I'm writing down Dan Monk," and I seen him scribbling. Monk all of a sudden looked scared.

Harp didn't know the half of them drovers,

but he stared at them one by one, scribbling doodles. And then the dangedest thing. That bunch began to run, each man for himself.

"He's taking names, he's taking names!" The words drove them away, drove them out of there, fleeing as if for their lives, away from the stink of it. They jumped onto their broncs, and grabbed Hook's broncs, including that roan of his. They saddled anything with four feet.

"I'm taking names," roared Francis Harp.

They scattered like hell was opening up behind them. Even Monk went white and fled, spurring his bronc like a crazy man. Ham Bark, too, spurring hard, looking as guilty as a cathouse token. They all clattered on down the lane, and hit the Sixteen Mile road, and beat hell out of their broncs getting away.

Harp stared at me stonily and shoved the paper into a pocket.

"Too late," he muttered.

"You saved the rest of us."

"Sam Hook is dead."

"God have mercy on him," boomed the preacher.

We'd forgotten Mr. Richard. I untied him and helped him down off his nag. He stood there stomping blood back into his feet and hands.

Then I done what I had to, in spite of the

putrification of my belly. I pushed my feet forward and walked myself over to Sam Hook, then cut him down with my jackknife, laid him gently on the ground, rolled his eyes shut, and put his head straight.

When I glanced up, there was Maud and Padlock and Jerome staring down, and night had fallen.

CHAPTER 13

Maud Wall – excuse me – Maud Hook sank down in her silvery blue wedding dress beside Sam Hook and gently, gently lifted his head into her lap and held it with both hands. She didn't cry. She just held his head, smoothed his hair, and stared vacantly into the murk of night, and then down upon her man who looked peaceful.

Padlock and Jerome paid their respects, black-eyed and silent, then stood aside guarding Maud and Sam. The preacher and Harp and me, we just sat off to one side and let nature run its course.

Maud sat that way for an hour or so, and just when I was wondering if she was going to sit that way all night, she slid out from Sam.

"We have loved, Sam," she said finally. And, "I'll do it."

She stood. As if by prearrangement, Padlock rolled Hook in a blanket and carried him on up to the house with the rest of us following. Jerome had disappeared somewhere.

"Please stay, all of you. I would like you here tonight, Mr. Oglesby."

"Gladly," I replied. I was planning to, anyway, just in case some of those bronco billies decided to return and make tribulation.

She began to set out food, cold beef and bread.

"I'll do that," I protested. "You rest, ma'am."

"It is better to keep busy."

But no one was much hungry.

Padlock had laid Sam Hook across the great oak desk and had pulled back the blanket from Sam's face so that he seemed to lie in state. Death had eased the muscles of Sam's face into serenity. And there he lay, dominating those silent people gathered there. Only Padlock stirred, stepping in and out upon the night, engaged in some business of his own. Once I heard the scrape of a shovel and I thought I knew what he was about.

Mr. Richard, who had come within an ace of death himself, slumped in a bullhide chair, drawn and silent. I could see Francis Harp thinking, his eyes darting around, his bony hand running through his dark hair.

Maud kept her own vigil, quiet at times, pacing restlessly at others. At the end of each pacing she stopped at the candlelit desk and stared wide-eyed at Sam Hook.

Once I seen her hand clench.

"I'll do it, Sam," she whispered. "You'd want me to."

In the middle of the night I heard a wagon rattle in the lane and, thinking trouble had come, began slamming shutters and damping out wicks. But just as I grabbed for Hook's Greener, Padlock stopped me.

"It's Jerome," he said.

Him and me plunged out into the night. The overcast was gone and I seen the Big Dipper tilted to midnight up there in the big sky, and I felt a fresh night breeze. Jerome was down to the pens unhitching and when we got there I seen it, the golden oak box of Widow Thwait's.

"They give it to you?"

"No one was there. The door was swinging open. It belongs to Sam, anyway."

"I suppose so," I agreed. "The widow got took up to Jethro's. How'd you know about the box?"

"Sam told us. And before that, I heard you tell Sam about it the night you came."

"Of course. You're looking after him good."

Padlock smiled at me in the lively dark. "He was our brother."

Them two carried the box into the house, but not into the big room. Instead, they turned off to Sam's bedroom. Padlock padded into the big room and half-apologetically said, "Excuse me," then lifted up Sam and carried him off.

No one said nothing.

A while later the pair of them hauled the box back in, slow and careful, and laid it on the desk. Sam was in it. And danged if I wasn't surprised. They had him in a fine buckskin shirt with quillwork. And on top of him they'd laid an eagle-plume warbonnet. No ordinary bonnet, neither. That thing was the finest bonnet I'd ever laid eyes on, each feather plucked from some sky-giant and anchored in a fine buckskin band with beadwork. The tail of it stretched down to Sam's feet and halfway back up again. That bonnet, that was for a chief of chiefs. It got me to wondering what Sam was among the Blackfeet. That was a part of his life nobody knew much about, except maybe them bucks. I made up my mind to find out some day.

Sam's Greener was in there too, and a fine sinew-wrapped bow and a doeskin quiver and arrows. I didn't know if that stuff was Sam's own, or whether them bucks were giving it to Sam now.

Maud peered in there and saw all that.

"You've honored Sam greatly," she said.

Some gentle light rose in Padlock's impassive face. "Our people named him Lifegiver. When the Indian agents starved us and stole our beef ration, Sam found food for us and kept many alive. He hunted through bitter winters, and browbeat the agents, and wrote letters to public authorities and somehow kept us fed and warm, at great cost to himself. We honored him with that name and these gifts."

"I didn't know. It is the same man who helped the young women. . . ."

Padlock drew himself up. "We will stay for the burial in the morning and then we will leave."

"I — what do you mean?"

"We are returning to our reservation."

"But why?"

"So as not to burden you further."

"I'm afraid I don't understand," Maud said. Francis Harp was staring now.

"This ranch is yours, Mrs. Hook. We wish to withdraw any claim to it," Padlock said.

"But — please call me Maud. And, Mr. Padlock, permit me to use your first name. I've never heard it spoken."

"There is none. My name is Padlock, keeper of wealth."

"I want you to take your shares. I won't have it, your leaving. Sam wanted you to have shares, gave you shares."

"Mrs. Hook —"

"Maud."

"Maud. Defending an Indian claim in a white-man court is a costly, losing proposition that would drag you and this ranch into debt. We wish to spare you a futile and expensive —"

"No!" bellowed Francis Harp.

Them bucks sure started when Francis Harp boiled out of his vigil chair.

"We'll not betray Sam Hook while he lies there still warm," Harp said. "I'm defending. And I'm defending the three of you jointly, the partnership. We'll be stronger, and I can do a better job, if you three hang together. And we'll not talk about fees for now."

"We'd feel more comfortable going back among our people. Indian wealth and white-man wealth are two different things."

"Would you leave a widow here to defend this property alone?" Harp pressed.

Maud said, "I need you both. I have promised Sam that I'd do it. I'd fight for this place. I will not turn over to barbarians this island of civilization that Sam built. I will fulfill his wishes and his dream."

"You have plans?" asked Harp.

"I am forming them. And they include my partners. Mr. Padlock, Jerome, if Sam was your brother, may I not be your sister?"

"Do you wish to be a sister of the Blackfeet?"

"I already am."

"It is done then."

Maud walked up to each of them and embraced them. Just like that. It made me squirmy but I didn't say nothing. She had her own way of doing things and if it included hugging Injuns, there was no stopping her.

Harp said, "You three face grave dangers. At the least the theft of your property. At the worst, death. And in between, every imaginable harassment by the powers that be who are eager to drive you off and confiscate all of this. They will use Mr. Oglesby here to impose their legal edicts."

"We'll talk of that some other time," replied Maud sharply.

But Harp had seen what was already on my mind. Summonses handed down to me to arrest them Injuns; court orders seizing the place and requiring me to padlock it. I had an oath of office binding me. The thing had already begun to bother me, and that old sot was reminding me how soon it was going to happen.

The next morning we buried Sam Hook. The Injuns had cut a grave into the hill above the house, beside a big juniper. The four of us

— Padlock, Jerome, Harp and me — carried the oak box up there, with Ormly Richard behind and Maud on his arm. She had no widow weeds but she'd wrapped herself in a black shawl. We eased Sam down into that hole first off and then climbed up to the daylight.

Mr. Richard didn't really know Hook none so he stayed pretty straight-and-narrow and led us through a prayer and them Scripture passages promising life hereafter, and so on, his great voice booming on down the slopes through the slanting sun and past the hanging tree far below.

He got to preaching about Hook being up there with the angels after a life well lived and I got to remembering Hook's jabber about Bark's dog being in doggy heaven, and I figgered maybe old Sam believed it all. Maybe he *was* up there, his old hazel eyes staring down at us, or maybe he was grinning that grin of his, the way he always done when he caught someone fudging. I hadn't much use for that heaven stuff myself but it had formed Hook, and maybe had helped him confront the Reaper more easy.

Then the preacher talked about the burying following the marrying and how them souls were still intertwined together, and I seen Maud's face go soft, not with pain, but with

180

happiness at the preacher's notion of them souls still hooked up for all eternity. It seemed like that was the only marriage she'd ever know now. Then Mr. Richard said another prayer and commended Sam Hook's soul to God and was done.

Maud dropped yesterday's daisies onto the box and them bucks shoveled the red clay back in until there was a raw red mound beside the juniper. Then we walked back down the hill. It was all over.

We all had to get on up to White Sulphur, except them bucks of course. The preacher and Maud and Harp climbed into the two-horse phaeton and I got into my buggy and we said our goodbyes to Padlock and Jerome. Me, I didn't figger ever to see them again. They'd either be dead within a few hours or off to the Blackfeet reservation. Or on the lam as outlaws because they'd get blamed for the horses we shot from the house in that fracas. But getting killed was most likely. They'd be out trying to save all that stock from wholesale theft, and sure as shooting they'd walk into an ambush set up by them bronco billies who'd shoot them and throw them into some coulee somewhere under a pile of rocks.

"I'll return with help," Maud told them, but I doubt they believed her. It was hard to figger what they'd do, but I sure knew what I'd do if I was an Injun with a hundred white men wanting me dead. I'd get. Last I seen, as the phaeton pulled out and me following, was them two staring at us white men.

We got to the ford of the South Fork and made it across, all of us silent. Harp and the preacher were all drawn down inside of themselves.

When we got to the fork where the road heads east toward the Castles, Maud tugged at the reverend until he stopped, and I stopped behind. She got out and came back to me.

"Is this the turnoff to Hamilton Bark's?" she asked.

"It is."

"How far?"

"Two miles or so. Not far."

"Are you in a hurry? Would you take me there?"

"Ma'am – Maud – you don't want to go there."

"Yes, I do. And I need an escort."

"No, I'm not taking you. A few hours ago Ham Bark was fixing to string you up. For all we know he still might be liquored and –"

"Please take me. It's another day now."

I protested all I could and then fetched her portmanteau from the phaeton and bid them two gents goodbye. I loaded up Maud and turned east with a gut full of crabs.

I was danged sure I didn't want to go there and I don't know how she snookered me into it, except she had that same kind of stare as Sam Hook.

We pulled into Bark's lane, me with a mess of butterflies in my belly.

"You stay here, ma'am and I'll just take your message on up there –"

She paid me no heed, stepped out, and marched up to that white house. I figgered he'd be too hung over to do a lick of work today and maybe the missus would shoo Maud off.

Maud knocked. There was a muffled snarl in there and the door flung open. Ham Bark stood there, unkempt, in red longjohns, pants, and suspenders, gawking at Maud.

"Well?"

Maud was pale and I thought I saw a tremor run through her.

"I've come to tell you I'll be at the spring roundup."

"What are you talking about?"

"I will rep for the Fishhook Ranch at the spring roundup."

"No, you won't. No women at roundups."

"I will be there as an owner."

"What the hell are you talking about now?"

"I am one of three partners who own the Fishhook. I have been for a year."

"Hook owned the Fishhook. It'll be up to the courts, lady."

"The Fishhook and its livestock will not be in probate because Sam Hook did not own a bit of it when he died. When he was murdered."

Bark's face oranged up bad. He was in an owly mood and not wanting nonsense from some crazy woman.

"Lady, you're not going to be at that roundup."

"You've no legal right to prevent me."

"I will kick your female behind out of there and keep on kicking."

"So that you can steal without witnesses? I will be there."

"Get out of here. Get out of this county or I'll throw you out."

"We'll see. I came here for another reason. To look at your face."

"What's my face —"

"I wanted to see what the face of a lyncher and murderer looks like the day after."

"Get out of here. Oglesby, get her out of this county by tomorrow or I'll kick you and her clear to Helena."

"Now, Ham," I said sociably, "Maud here's a little upset is all. You just relax and we'll get this roundup business all squared away some other time. I don't figger she means it, associating with all them rough drovers."

"Mr. Oglesby, I will not relish the company, but I'll be there. Mr. Bark, my attorney has written down your name."

"What's that got to do with — get out. Get off my land."

"Mr. Harp has written down the names of all those who murdered Sam. He has written down your name."

Hamilton Bark barged through the door like a bull, swung a roundhouse right, and smashed a fist into Maud's cheek. She flew backward into a heap, and then hugged her head, barely conscious.

"Get back, Ham, dammit," I yelled. "Get into your house or I'll have you on assault and battery."

"Out of my way fatso. That lady needs a lesson she'll never forget." He grinned.

I heard the click of a hammer cocking behind me and I seen Bark suddenly go quiet.

"Don't move a muscle, Ham," said a soft voice behind me, and I turned to see Win Coop standing there, a mean fowling piece aimed at Bark.

"Draw your pay and get out," Bark said to him. "That's twice in two days,

Coop. You're through here."

"Don't move your mouth muscles either," said Win.

Maud was on her knees, rocking back and forth and biting back tears.

"All right, Bark. Turn your back and walk to the house. I'll be out of here in ten minutes."

Bark turned slow, walked slow, and then slammed the door behind him.

Win helped Maud up and got her brushed off. Her lips were mashed and bloody and her cheek was showing signs of a bruise.

"I'll help you to the buggy, ma'am. It's Mrs. Hook now, isn't it? And if the Fishhook is looking for a seasoned hand and ex-foreman, I'm available."

Maud managed a smile. "Mr. Harp tells me that anyone connected with the Fishhook is in mortal danger. If that still suits you, you're hired. I'll let Mr. Padlock know, or rather, you can tell him I have employed you."

"I'll get my gear and be over there soon." Win turned to me. "No one in town —"

"I figgered as much. You did your best and I admire that you tried."

Win turned to Maud again. "Mrs. Hook, repping at the roundup isn't going to help you any. This morning, with Sam Hook dead, every ranch in the valley sent out crews to rope and brand Fishhook calves. In a day or two there won't be a longhorn calf paired to a Fishhook cow. Those calves will all disappear. And when they show up in the fall, not a one of them will carry a Fishhook brand."

Maud nodded. "All the more reason for me to rep at the roundup."

"You'd better plan on my being there and repping for you. They'd chase you off and they'd kill your Blackfeet."

"Please tell that to Mr. Padlock," she said. "And thank you, Mr. Coop."

We drove on to White Sulphur, Maud and I. I can't say as I liked that woman any more than I liked Sam Hook. They were two of a kind, independent and not the sort to get along with folk. But she was a strong one. And after going through the hell of last night, we had some sort of bond that made me enjoy having her on that buggy seat beside me.

It was a fine spring afternoon and the sun was working up the scent of the sagebrush.

"Mind if I ask a question, Maud?"

"Ask it and I'll tell you whether I mind."

"How come you and Sam — how come you took so long. Him and you, it's been years now."

"I was the one who resisted. I've found a life, a vocation, I cherish. I had no wish to surrender a work that has salvaged scores of lives and brought new life into the world, new life with a good chance for happiness. And I had no wish to live at a lonely country ranch."

"Then how did you —"

"Sam was more flexible. He finally proposed that I stay where I am and continue to do what I do, and he'd shuttle back and forth. It made him happy. He loved my vocation."

She smiled wanly.

"You see, Sam saw the frontier ending. He saw needs, such as the desperation of the women I help. Mr. Oglesby, he spanned the whole frontier, from the days when he trapped in a virgin land to now, when people are settling and building towns. He never looked back or pined for the old ways."

"What'll you do now?" I asked.

"Mr. Oglesby, I don't know."

CHAPTER 14

I told them leading lights — Judge Bark, Clyde Park, and Clay Cott — the whole story as exact as I could make it, there in the Sherman Hotel saloon. Them ravens, they listened close and sharp-eyed, sucking on sourmash.

"A pity. We lost one of the county's leading lights. There was no more public-spirited stockman than Bert Stern," proclaimed Jefferson Bark. "And of course old Hook. A bad business."

"A great loss, Stern," agreed Clyde Park. "But I think Hook did us a favor."

That line of reasoning was a puzzle to the rest of us.

"If Hook hadn't shot Stern when he did, that mob — er, group — would have strung up that preacher. And that would have put me on the griddle. Our good citizens wouldn't stand for that — hanging Ormly Richard — and they'd have demanded action, and fast. Warrants, arrests. I'd have had to issue warrants for the whole south half of the county. As it is, there's no problem. Hook shot Stern. Hook's dead. The preacher is alive." He grinned. "Swift justice."

Amen to that, I thought. The idea of arresting all them stockmen and bronco billies down there made my blood run cold.

Clyde Park drummed his pink fingers on the table, and then fixed me with them white eyes. Only man I ever seen with all-white eyes, and just two black lens holes.

"I'll write warrants for those Indians and you go bring them in," he said.

"Warrants? For what?"

"Destroying livestock – they shot horses. Attempted murder – they put bullets into two or three people. Conspiracy to murder Bert Stern. Theft of a coffin. And a few other things."

"Whoa up," I said. "They were acting in pure self-defense. And they didn't conspire to shoot Stern. As for shooting them horses and putting bullets into them buckaroos trying to start the house on fire, that was to save their own lives, and the rest of us in there."

Park eyed me glacially. "Are you defending bucks now, Oglesby? I will prepare the warrants. You will arrest them. A duly constituted jury in Judge Bark's court will decide their guilt or innocence."

"You're going against the evidence," I muttered. I knew it would come to this.

Judge Bark hammered the table, as if he was in court banging with a gavel. "Your conduct in this entire business has been reprehensible, Oglesby," he snapped. "You should not have been inside that ranchhouse shooting at innocent citizens. You should have been outside. If there was any threat of a lynching earlier in the confrontation, you should have placed Hook and Maud Wall in protective custody and brought them swiftly here. You certainly should not have backed Hook or blinked at the theft of a coffin. I'm afraid I'm forced to prepare a case of malfeasance against you. Or rather, County Attorney Park will, and a grand jury will hear it. Unless, of course, you begin cooperating immediately with elected officers of this county."

That sure took me back some, and riled me up fast.

"They weren't innocent citizens. They were liquored up crazy men, planning on murder."

"There's no evidence of that," Bark snapped. "They'd come to make sure Hook was arrested for killing Widow Thwait, and when you failed to do your duty like a man, they grew a little unruly. . . ."

There was no use arguing with all them brainheads, and me just a sheriff.

"It's not Maud Wall, it's Maud Hook," I muttered.

"That's open to debate," snapped Park. "The courts will probably find that Hook was not of sound mind, and annul it."

"He was sound," I argued, feeling stubborn. "I'll testify to it and so will the preacher and Harp. Hook was just as sane as any of us setting here." I don't know what was getting into me but I was plumb mad, and itching to tangle with them.

Judge Bark smiled thinly. "Expert testimony will determine that. It is not a question that can be settled by the uneducated opinion of a sheriff, or a drunken lawyer, or a preacher who'd barely met Hook. There will be many witnesses to the contrary, Mr. Oglesby. Your opinion is totally irrelevant, out of bounds and, I might add, insubordinate."

"Maybe so," I said. "But Hook's dead. Them longhorns are on their way out, I figger. There ain't no problems anymore, so why not leave it alone?"

"Because justice's not yet done," declared Clyde Park. "It is plain that those Indians and that gold-digging Wall woman conspired to defraud and bilk an unstable old man, and apparently succeeded after buttering up Hook for years. This county is vitally concerned with protecting Hook's large estate from such theft. I am preparing a suit alleging fraud and freezing Hook's estate. It will seek to nullify the transfer of Hook's property to the conspirators, nullify the will, and I'll make sure it nullifies the fake marriage as well."

"But you wrote up that will when you were Hook's attorney!"

"Ah, indeed, and it was a sorrow, knowing the old man was not of sound mind. And, yes, that reminds me: I will also have Harp thrown out. Employing the drunk was in itself a mark of Hook's senility. I shall have myself reinstated as conservator of Hook's estate. Hook was, after all, concealing his conduct from me while I was his counselor, and secretly conveying his property to a partnership, knowing I'd oppose."

"Maybe that ain't the right interpretation," I glowered.

"What are you suggesting, Sheriff?" Park glared back.

"Maybe Hook figgered you weren't being proper with him."

"I see," Park said. Him and Jeff Bark exchanged looks. Clay Cott smiled too. "You seem to be questioning my integrity."

I didn't say nothing.

Clay Cott spoke up. "You know, Clyde, you're taking the long way around, all this law, and endless suits. Harp will resist every step of the way as Maud Wall's attorney. Meanwhile the property will lose value. I'd hate to see a prime ranch run down."

"So?"

"So, suggest an arrangement, a buy-out, with perhaps a little pressure to induce the alleged partners to come around. Invite Maud Wall and the Indians to surrender their interest, cede it to probate, and agree that Hook died intestate and without issue."

Park beamed. "In exchange for dropping charges. Indeed. And clearing out of Meagher County. Worth a try, Clay. Maybe this will do it." He lifted a document from his vestpocket and handed it to me. It was a court order, signed by Judge Bark, declaring Maud's place a public nuisance and ordering it closed in five days. I stared hard at all them words.

"Ah, Mr. Oglesby, here indeed is a task for you. Convey this to Maud Wall and invite her to surrender her interest in the Hook estate. If she does, tell her that perhaps this order can be lifted. I'm sure Judge Bark here is quite willing to reconsider. And go talk with those Blackfeet and let them know I'm preparing charges, but that I'm willing to drop them if they cooperate on the Hook estate."

"I'll think on it," I said.

"What do you mean by that?"

"It doesn't sound legal to me, threatening them with charges and all."

"Sheriff Oglesby, you shall do your duty. If you defy proper authority you might yourself be committing a criminal offense. You'd be dismissed and disgraced and face a term at Deer Lodge."

Well, there it was. I could keep my star, long as it was potmetal. They figgered me for a potmetal sheriff.

"I understand perfect," I said. "That there Hook property needs protecting. I'm going to be going on down to that spring roundup and make sure all them longhorn calves tally up and them longhorn bulls are accounted for."

That sort of silenced them some.

"I think . . ." began Judge Bark, "that's not really sheriff business. The stockmen have brand inspectors for that sort of thing."

"I'm going. Rustling's a sheriff matter and if I catch any buckaroo or stockman down there mavericking, why I'll —"

"Oglesby, that's very noble, but other matters are more pressing. You must deal with this conspiracy of Maud Wall and the Indians against the Hook estate," said Clay Cott.

"I'm for protecting the property of the deceased. Guess I'll just mosey on down there and poke around ahead of the roundup."

"We need you here," said Judge Bark.

"Jethro'll look after things."

"As you wish," said Park, looking daggers at me.

"Fact is, I'm going to deputize Win Coop. He's on the Hook place and I'll empower him to nab anyone tries to grab any property, four-legged or otherwise."

"That's not necessary." Judge Bark looked dyspeptic. "He's an unreliable man, that's obvious from his conduct toward Hamilton. In fact, Clyde, he threatened to shoot Ham. That's a criminal offense. Prepare a warrant and have Oglesby here go down there and bring him in." He eyed me. "If you should resist or fail, Oglesby . . ."

"I hear you."

These here town fathers weren't leaving anything to chance. I figgered I'd better talk to Harp about whether they were drawing me into extortion or something. And I sure had better have a sit-down with Maud. I wished I had kept my big mouth shut about Win.

"Anyone I should deputize and put on the

Hook place other than Win?" I asked.

Clyde Park beamed whitely. "Why yes, I believe so. There's a fine fellow works for Stern and Monk ... Lorenzo Strunck's his name. I hear good things of him. Why, yes. Deputize Strunck if you will."

"Whatever you say."

"You run along on this errand to Wall's now, Oglesby. By the time you get back I'll have papers ready for the rest."

Errand boy, that's what they thought of me. I got up to go.

"Oh, Oglesby," said Judge Bark. "The county's sending a splendid funeral wreath over to Stern's ranch. Your share is five dollars."

"Out of my fifty a month?"

"That's your share, Oglesby."

I buzzed out of that Sherman Hotel in one hurry, stewing as I stalked east toward Maud's. I didn't know what had happened to this whole sheriff business since the Hook trouble started. I didn't know what I'd tell Maud, neither. My mind kept jumping back to the sight of Hook hanging and choking and mouthing them last two words, Love Maud, and it got me sick just thinking. Unless a man's mean as an alligator, he sees a hanging once and never wants to see another.

I thought maybe I should resign. But they'd

just appoint someone who'd follow orders better than me. Worse than me. I didn't like thinking I'd done a bad job, but the thought was in my head. *Worse than me.* I remembered what I had told Molly — I'd been bought and sold.

When I got to Maud's I knocked.

She opened the door and said, "Sheriff Oglesby, come in. Mr. Harp is here."

Sure enough, there was the gaunt lawyer balancing one of them Spode teacups on his knee. I told them the whole of it and showed them the court order.

"Baseless. Scandalous. Faulty procedure," Harp muttered. "A scandalous document and an extortion threat — surrender the Hook property or we'll shut your place down as a public nuisance."

He paced through the parlor, hands clasped behind his back.

"Tell me the rest again. What they are planning. The alleged conspiracy to defraud Hook."

I told them what Clyde Park had in mind.

Maud sat there pale in widow's weeds. I supposed them girls were upstairs.

"It's bad law, poor procedure, patent nonsense. Unfortunately Judge Bark would be sitting in judgment of it all. . . ." He glared at me. "Sheriff Oglesby, it's time for you to take a stand. Where do you stand? What side are you on?"

"Why, I want to do my duty, ah . . ."

"That's not what I asked. Tell me as a man: where do you stand?"

I figgered the moment of truth had come. There wasn't no way I could escape it. I unpinned the star and handed it to Harp.

"See that? Everyone calls it a tin star, but it's some kind of potmetal. I hear some rich counties have real silver stars. This one's potmetal, and I been a potmetal sheriff."

Harp glanced sharply at me. "I don't care what you've been. I've been a drunk and such a bad lawyer I've destroyed clients. I want to know what you intend to be."

"I'd like to be a good lawman. But it's too late. I'm the way I am, and they're getting up charges against me. . . ."

Well, that got Harp going. He wanted to know what the malfeasance charges were all about, so I told him all about that and the trouble I was in.

"I got my sworn duty to enforce the law and do like Judge Bark and that county attorney say, or they'll pack me off."

Harp, he just sighed. "There's real law and there's Park-and-Bark law, coyote law." He guffawed a moment. "All you have to do is enforce the real law, and forget about their law. They'll threaten and roar, but not too much because exposure could destroy them. Don't forget they're dependent on you. They have no way to enforce their edicts without you and no fast way to get rid of you without a three-ring circus first. You do what's right and I'll worry about the rest. Mr. Oglesby, you'll do fine."

He called me mister, the same as Sam Hook did when I went down there to warn him about the widow. I wasn't used to nobody calling me that.

Harp said, "Maud, I think it would be wise for you to close this establishment temporarily. You and your charges would be safer at the ranch. Why not move there in four or five days, just before this order —"

"But I can't, Francis. Constance is well into her ninth month. Dr. Easum will be too far if I should need him."

Harp persisted. "If you plan to attend the roundup with Win Coop, you'd best have your young ladies close at hand, at the ranch. You can't leave the ladies here in White Sulphur while you're there."

That decided it. I could see that. Maud had to head down there with the women or forget repping at the roundup.

"I'll go," she said. "I'll need a few days. And

I'll need to make arrangements with Dr. Easum. You're right, Francis. I'd feel more protected just now at the ranch with Jerome, Padlock, and Win Coop."

"I figger you should stay here," I said. "It don't make sense to jump every time Park and them snap their fingers. The more you jump, the more they'll snap fingers. There ain't anything can happen if you stay put."

Francis Harp stopped his pacing and walked to me, kind of friendly. "It's for your sake, Will," he said.

"My sake!"

"Yes, your sake. Sometime soon I'll discuss it with you. Not now."

"You mean because of all that malfeasance in office stuff?"

"We'll talk about it later, Will."

"I've got to take a message back to Clyde Park. What do I tell him?"

Harp and Maud exchanged a glance.

"Tell Park that Maud says no; she will not relinquish her rightful share in the partnership or her widow's claim in the will, if the partnership should be found to be null."

"I'll tell him."

I went back over to Park and told him no dice. He looked like he was sucking pickles.

I wasn't no sheriff; I was *everyone*'s errand boy.

It was getting late, and I figgered maybe to have me some sourmash and a steak over to Molly's and maybe Molly for dessert. I went on over wanting to talk but she was in one of her crab-apple moods and I might just as well have yapped at a stone wall. I always felt I should get my three dollars back when she acted like that. I needed someone to talk to. I didn't like the way my life was going. Everything had been fine until this Hook business and now I was on the edge of throwing it all to hell, getting stiff-necked instead of getting along with folks the way I used to. I was pitching away my whole future, seemed like, and I didn't understand why.

I hung around Molly's until late, getting more and more skunked, hating all them people pressuring me. Hating the job; hating the star. Hating Hook. Hating the trip tomorrow to arrest them bucks and Win Coop. I finally forced myself out into the night air and sucked it in, fresh and clean.

Off to the east the whole sky was oranged up bad. Fire, I figgered. Maybe . . . I began doubling that way, afraid of what that orange might mean. Sure enough, against the black sky Maud's house on that hill was an inferno. I heard the firebell then and I seen people grabbing buckets and axes, but I didn't grab a pail or nothing. I just run east up that slope, dreading what I'd find.

CHAPTER 15

The house stood on a rise well east of town, and by the time I got there, along with them other night owls, it was pretty much gone. Frame houses go fast.

The women were safe. Maud stood there calm and flint-eyed in her wrapper, with them girls in flannel nightgowns, the orange light shining through making leg shadows on the cloth. The chubby one, Constance, she was far along, I could see that. She was crying some, and the other, Caroline, was snuffling.

There was nothing anyone could do except watch the last of it collapse in showers of sparks. I saw that the women had dragged a lot out of there — dresses and blankets and things, which lay in a few heaps.

"It started while I was preparing for bed, Mr. Oglesby. On three sides at once."

I could see some kerosene cans lying around, left deliberate, it seems like, so there'd be no mistake that some one or two or three had torched that place.

"I awakened my young ladies and there was enough time to gather a few things."

"Not much, I figger."

"Not much. The medical library's gone."

"What's that — a library?"

"My husband's. I mean, Professor Wall's. He was a professor of medicine, in the east. Dr. Easum used those books constantly. 'They're a godsend,' he told me. 'With these I can practice the best medicine in the Territory.' "

I didn't know what to say to that. I watched some of the others stroke the pump and pour a few pails of water here and there, but it was wasted effort and done nothing but make steam.

"Now they're gone," she said. "Along with my midwifing things."

She seemed too calm. I wished she would cry or scream or something instead of being all buttoned up inside.

"This wasn't no warning," I opined. "Someone wanted you dead pretty bad."

"Of course. I'm Mrs. Hook now."

"I figger them Injuns are in for it, too."

She sighed. "I'd like your help. We need to be taken to the Fishhook. We have no place else. I'm sure Francis Harp will help, too."

Constance was wailing so Maud slipped over there, hugged that girl, and said things I couldn't hear with all the crackle of that orange fire, but the young woman calmed down and pretty soon Maud come back to me.

"You sure you want to go down there? Safer here, maybe."

"Mr. Coop is there now, in addition to Mr. Padlock and Jerome."

"That girl stand the trip?"

"She's splendidly healthy."

"I'm going in the morning. I've, uh, business there anyway. I can take you in my buggy and them girls can come along in Harp's one-horse trap. He's skinny."

"You have business?"

"Yes." Dang, how could I tell her I was going to arrest them bucks and Coop too? Or at least threaten them bucks like Park wanted.

"Well," she said bitterly, "this will spare you the unpleasant task of shutting this place down in five days. Your 'public nuisance' has burned down."

"It ain't my public nuisance, ma'am."

"I'm cold," whimpered Caroline.

Maud rummaged through the pile and found a blanket. Them other people were staring at them girls like they'd never seen a woman in a delicate condition before.

"You all go back to town now," I shouted. "I'll handle this. Thanks for your help. This fire ain't going anywhere except out."

I could see a lot of them people were there to watch the women, not the fire, and they weren't budging.

"Maud, you got any valuables in your sheds?"

"Very little. Some preserves in the root cellar, some harnesses and gardening tools and a grindstone."

"Let's get you out of here. You and these girls are getting stared at."

She nodded.

The women loaded a couple of portmanteaus they'd salvaged, while I toured the grounds, getting a good look at the jaspers standing around. Sometimes burners came back to watch the show, so I wanted to memorize faces. But I can't say as I saw anyone from any ranch. Just town people is all. I gathered up the kerosene cans as evidence.

"Let's get," I growled. I handed Caroline the cans. "You take these and and I'll get the bags."

"Where are we going?" Maud asked.

"The Sherman Hotel."

"But I have no — my reticule burned. . . ."

"I'll take care of that, dang it."

So off we went. Two barefoot girls, one in a blanket, the other in her flannel, and Maud in her wrapper.

It was late when we marched into the lobby, which was dark and shadowy except for one hanging oil lamp. I banged the bell because there wasn't no one at the desk. It took some right smart banging, but after a while Smoot himself came out, sour-looking, and gave the bunch of us the cold eye.

"Two rooms," I said.

"I'm full." He turned around.

"Whoa up," I snarled. "Get these ladies into two rooms."

He drew himself up like he was about ready to spit. "We don't let rooms to single women of dubious morals," said he, all puffed up.

Well, that plain steamed me up, after the fire and all. That Smoot was built like a wide blacksmith but I grabbed him by the front of his bathrobe and yanked.

"These here women got burnt out. You give them two rooms. One for the girls and one for Mrs. Wall — Mrs. Hook, here."

"By what authority —"

"By sheriff authority, by God. That's what, or you'll by damn spend the night over to the jail."

"And just who will pay?"

"We'll dang well worry about that later. You dang well better give me keys or I'll dang well march you down the street."

I loosened my grip on that big cowpie and he gave me looks fit to kill a buffalo herd, but then he slid me two keys.

"Fourteen and fifteen," Smoot said. "And I want them out by eight."

"I'll fetch them when I'm ready and they're ready," I snarled.

Then I toted them portmanteaus to the rooms.

"Thank you, Sheriff," said Maud.

"Maud, ma'am, before you get away, I got to look into this. Do you know who done this? Anything you remember peculiar about it?"

She thought for a moment. "No, I have no clue. But it was not many hours ago that Mr. Bark struck me after learning that I was a part owner of the Fishhook."

She put her finger on it. "I'll look around in the morning," I said.

"I have a question for you, Sheriff. You never told me what your business is at the Fishhook."

Dang, I didn't want to answer that. "I'll talk about it in the morning. Maybe it won't happen."

She stared at me peculiar, with that cat-eye look I didn't like none. In the lamplight I seen how bruised her cheek was.

"Good night, ladies," I said. I collected the cans, dropped them at the jailhouse, and walked to my shack south of Main Street for some shuteye.

I was up before dawn. I wanted to have a good look at Maud's place before all the gawkers showed up. It was going to be a fine summery day. The air was transparent and clear when the sun broke open, clean and fresh as a new diaper. I wolfed down some flapjacks, buckled on my six-gun, and got up there maybe five or five-thirty with the sky going white before it settled blue. The place stank of char and a few wisps of smoke still curled up here and there. I trudged around the mess careful, but there was nothing. No bootprints. I found some nails and a hammer in the shed and nailed the shed door shut to slow down vandals. I poked around some more off a ways, looking for hoofprints, but there was nothing except the mixed-up ones on the road.

I knew pretty well Ham Bark done it, but I didn't have anything to go with, and even if I had something solid, there wasn't much I could do. I just stood there pensive, staring down at White Sulphur, watching the slanting sun hit the east sides of all the town buildings. Funny, I'd never noticed how Maud's place had a view of the town.

Pretty soon Clyde Park would be breakfasting down there and waiting for me to pick up the blamed papers. It was a pretty town in the dawn light, even if worms were crawling through it.

I sat down in the bunchgrass just staring and fretting about the coming day. A skinny black figure started laboring up the slope toward me and after a while I recognized Francis Harp, out and about all-fired early. He stared at the black ruins and then settled down beside me on the grass as if it was some regular day and we were having a picnic.

"I've never seen White Sulphur from this prospect at this hour," he said. "Enchanting. A virgin town in a virgin territory."

He eyed me slaunchwise.

"Maud told me. None of them rested, of course. I have a trap and harness and will rent a driving horse from Tin Flynn. I had a good horse once, but . . . lost it as a result of my weaknesses."

"I've got to wait two or three hours."

"Maud said you had business at the Fishhook."

I didn't say nothing.

"I'm discomforting you. I suppose what I'll do is get Tin busy and then drive the young ladies. You and Maud can follow in a few hours when you're ready."

He was staring at me.

211

My head was a mess and I wasn't making heads or tails of anything.

"You have your duty to do and have sworn an oath of office," the gaunt old boy rattled on. "That's an excellent thing — do what must be done, Mr. Oglesby."

I was starting to get the drift of what he was planning to do. "Your going on ahead of me ain't gonna solve anything. Maybe just delay," I said.

"It is too early for solutions," he replied. "For now I will improvise day by day." He rose up on those long bony legs. "I will have the young ladies safely ensconced by the time you and Maud arrive," he assured me and he tottered off down the slope.

I sat there a long time, an hour maybe, thinking I should resign. Sheriffing was a job I didn't want no more. But danged if I didn't keep thinking of Sam Hook and it was like Sam telling, me, Don't do it, Will — you just keep working at being a good sheriff and let the chips fall where they will.

I wasn't much of a sheriff, no matter what Hook's ghost was whispering at me, and I didn't know whether I wanted to be one. Good sheriffs get themselves shot at or fired or voted out all too regular, I figgered.

That rig of Harp's crawled south and out of

sight and pretty soon I dusted off my britches and went on down there to Clyde Park's office.

Park was in rare good humor and he grinned at me until his pink gums gleamed.

"The abatement went ahead of schedule, I hear," he chortled. "Here's your papers."

He handed me three warrants. Felony charges for the Injuns; high misdemeanor for Win.

"You will of course bring them all in."

"If I can catch them, and that's God's truth. If they ain't handy, I'll have some chasing to do."

"You can raise a posse."

"I just might have to."

"Where's Maud Wall?"

"Hook."

"Don't be silly. Wall."

"The hotel."

"Keep her there. I'm filing arson charges."

"Arson! She set out to kill herself and them girls, did she?"

"Who knows what she tried to do. There were kerosene cans around and I hear she conveniently got everything out of the house."

I got out of there fast.

In no time we were trotting south, me and Maud, and it was some while before I began to relax. I crossed the plank bridge over the North

Fork and headed on down the west side of the Smith valley for a change.

"Park's gonna file arson charges against you, Maud," I said at last.

"Why? Because I'm Sam Hook's widow?"

I sighed. "That, and to sow confusion in folks' minds, and put more heat on you. This thing keeps growing. It started as a row among them ranchers about Hook's bulls and now that Sam Hook's buried, it seems like everyone wants a slice of what's left."

"What evidence does Clyde Park have?"

"He doesn't need evidence, Maud. This is just a railroad job in Jeff Bark's court. Likely aimed to scare you out of the county."

"I imagine they will succeed."

"You scared?"

"Yes, terribly. Last night was an attempt to murder us, not frighten us."

"Why do you say that?"

"We escaped from the back door. All the other sides were aflame. There was kerosene smell at the back, too — I saw a puddle — but they had fled. . . ."

"You didn't say nothing about that."

"I didn't think to tell you last night. I was . . . upset. And it didn't have meaning until I relived the terror of it over and over last night."

"Maybe you and them girls should move to Helena."

She sighed. "Maybe I'll have to. But I made a promise. I told Sam . . . I'd try."

"Get yourself killed, is what you'll do. Them bucks too. All three of you partners."

"That puzzles me. What good would it do? I mean if we were dead or driven away? Sam Hook had no heirs – except for me – and the ranch would go to the Territory, wouldn't it? I don't understand who'd benefit."

"Maud – ma'am – it's not a matter of benefiting. It's a matter of hating. They hated Hook. They hate rich Injuns even worse. And even worse than that, a no-nonsense woman who ends up both a partner and Hook's widow. And besides, there's plenty of benefit. The Territory will turn it over to the county to sell, and one of them buzzards will get it cheap, with Clay Cott financing it and getting a cut. And they'll grab the livestock for sure."

"Hate? It's hard to imagine."

"Hate and fear and greed," I said. "You and them Injuns were witnesses, you know. You could holler to the whole world what you seen there, the hanging, the stringing up of that preacher almost, all that. It ain't them long-horns that's riling them, anymore. It's silence they want. They can't stand the thought of you jabbering to the paper or the public. Them people will do anything — like killing you in a fire."

"But — but Mr. Oglesby, there were three other witnesses. Mr. Richard, Francis Harp . . . and you. Wouldn't they want — to silence you, too?'

"You figgered it right, ma'am," I growled.

We drove through a sunburst of a day with the greening slopes warm under the big sky. Funny how you escape into Creation in this Territory and peace sneaks into you. We passed Grassy Mountain in a reverie, and Horse Butte too.

Actually I was keeping my eye wide open for trouble, but I wasn't telling her that. I was looking for any sign of trouble upon Harp, too, but I figgered he drove down the east side of the South Fork. I half expected to get to the Fishhook and find him and them girls never showed up.

We got to the Fishhook without incident and I seen Harp's rig and I figgered things were okay for the moment. I knew that Harp would've seen to it that them Injuns would be gone, so I dropped Maud at the verandah and wheeled toward the pens, fixing to unhook the bay. But Win Coop was there. I had expected him to be gone. The wiry foreman took the bay off my hands.

"They're at the house waiting for you. I'll be there in a moment," he said.

"Thanks, Win."

I stared at the man, thinking of that warrant. And also of that other surprise in my pocket that I picked up at the jailhouse before leaving. And I knew right there, standing in that Fishhook corral, that I'd come to some continental divide in the life of Wilbur Oglesby. I wasn't sure which way the water would run, but I knew I'd have to start toward some Atlantic or Pacific, and my life would never be the same. Maybe it was fitting that the choice came here on old Hook's place. He was the one put me in this mess. He was the one who might still get me killed. He was the one who mouthed his last words at me, Love Maud. And he was the one called me mister and meant something by it. I waited for Win and walked up to that big house with him.

There we were, the whole army, except for them Injuns. Maud and old Harp, temporarily sober, two big-bellied women, and Coop, against a dozen stockmen, two or three dozen hardcases and bronco billies, all handy with six-guns. That plus the bank, the court, the merchants, and the leading lights of White Sulphur.

Folks was sort of humming around in there. The women had got settled and were pulling out chow. Harp, he kept watching me like he was waiting for something. Win, he paced around the windows, not wanting surprises I guess.

There came a time when I had to do it and danged if my heart wasn't thumping and my belly sweating.

"Win Coop," I said.

He stared at me peculiar.

"Win, this place needs guarding. Them cattle are gonna disappear. Equipment'll vanish from these here buildings. The wells and tanks might be fouled. Who knows? The county needs a man here to keep an eye on this place. Whoever does it, his life ain't gonna be worth a dang. You think you're the man?"

Win, he just nodded. The girls were standing nearby and I seen Win and Constance exchange a glance – I got hit in the gut with a notion, but I put it aside.

"Raise your hand, Win. You solemn swear to uphold law in Montana Territory?"

"Sure do," he said.

I pinned the deputy badge on him and gave him a commission I had drawn up.

"You're a lawman now. Use it proper."

He grinned.

"Win," I continued, "I got sent down here by Clyde Park. He's trumped up some warrants against them bucks, and tells me I got to bring them in. You willing to go fetch them with me now?"

The face of Winfrid Coop was something not to behold. I watched a sadness settle on him and I seen the folk in that room all go tense. Harp was glaring at me.

"I think I'll resign the commission," said Win, soft as a cloud.

I handed him another paper. "Read that, Win. Park's trumped up a warrant against you for pulling iron on Ham Bark when he was pounding Maud. You think maybe you should arrest yourself as your first act?"

There was plain pain in his eyes. "I swore to uphold the law," he muttered.

"That's right. You're going to uphold the law and that piece of horseapple in your hand ain't law and neither are them phony warrants."

Win, that was too much for him, but Harp, he came barreling up and clamped his skinny paw in mine.

"You've crossed your Rubicon," he said.

"What's that mean?"

"Well, the Rubicon was a boundary that the Roman senate had forbidden Julius Caesar to

cross . . . It means you've made a fateful deci-
sion."

"Put me in Deer Lodge, I figger."

"No. It's the beginning of law in Meagher
County. Park and Bark will rage like lions but
they are helpless without you."

"They ain't helpless," I objected. "They got
teeth."

CHAPTER 16

Spring roundup had started and I figgered I'd better get down there and keep an eye on things. Maud was planning on being there and the stockmen hated the very thought of it.

I loaded camping gear into the buggy. I don't like camping none – it's hard on my shuteye. But I figgered it came with the job. I didn't say nothing to anyone in town. I just let Jethro know I'd be gone awhile, moseying around. I never said a word to Clyde Park. Let him think whatever he wanted. He sure glared at me when I came back from Hook's without a bunch of prisoners in cuffs but I kept my yap shut. I hoped they'd figger I was heading out now to round up the fugitives.

The communal roundup always started up north of town and worked south down to the low divide between the Smith and Shields valleys. From there the drovers would push the sale cattle, mostly culls in the spring, on down to the Northern Pacific pens at Livingston, about fifty miles south of there. I figgered

Maud wouldn't bother with the north-valley gather; few of them longhorns wandered up there. But she sure would be on hand when they got further south, in Hook's range. So I headed south, knowing I'd find the gather somewhere below Bark's place. It was there, all right. A man could hardly miss it with all that bawling and bellowing.

It was sure an owly camp, and the reason was plain enough. It wasn't only Maud there; it was them two big-bellied women, too, and one of them looking like she'd pop any second. Win had drove them over in a sheepwagon of Hook's, and that added insult to injury as far as the cattlemen were concerned. I didn't know how the three fit into there. Sheepwagons are little marvels. Under the bows and canvas is a whole little house with even a cookstove. There might be room for two, but three in there made it a mob.

Neither were them women staying put in that wagon. Maud was round and about with a pencil and paper and every time she saw a longhorn cow with a full dripping bag and no calf, she wrote it down and got the names from Coop of the drovers who brought it in.

I never seen such a mad bunch of men in my life. Soon as I got there, Stapp and Jung came snarling at me.

"If you don't get those women out of here, we will," yelled Stapp.

"She's an owner. It's public grass. She's got every right to be here," I retorted. "And I'm here to enforce that right."

"This gather's gone to hell because of those women," Jung snapped. "And we by God are going to drag them out if you don't."

"I'll arrest the first one who does or harms them in any way," I yelled back. "She's an owner. She's tallying same as you. And besides that, Widow Thwait was here every roundup."

"I don't care about rights, fatso, and I don't care about sheriff law either. They're about to get hurt; do you understand?"

"I don't see no longhorn calves around. Seems to me she ought to stay here and protect her property. From whoever. If she's being stole blind, taking down names might be the way to stop it."

"You get out!" yelled Stope. "You and those damned women, get out!"

"Sorry, Stope, I'm staying. I'm making my own notes and maybe I'll make some arrests too, with all this stealing."

He whirled away, disgusted, and began hollering at Maud, shoving her away from the branding. Them drovers were hot, too. Some had got burned; one had busted an arm; several calves had died; and they were all blaming the women.

I stood my ground, taking glare from the bronco billies. And I began to do my own note-scratching. I seen not one longhorn bull and not one longhorn calf, so I wrote the names of the drovers bringing in the bunches, at least the names I knew.

Dan Monk come over and ripped the paper out of my hands, and then before I could yell, he did the same to Maud, who went white but didn't say nothing. He dropped it in the fire where the irons were reddening up. The notes flared and smoked and he grinned.

"I see what I see, whether it's writ down or not, Dan," I said, mild as I could. "I could put cuffs on you for that, but I came to keep the peace here so we'll just forget it." The truth was, I was afraid to tangle with Dan Monk. He knew it and laughed.

Win and that little Constance, they seemed to hang together, talking a lot, and I suspicioned I knew who the daddy of that child was. Any time any drover began to yell at her, Win would bull in with fists ready and a red look in his eye that was pure respect-making.

"Maud," I said, "this ain't safe. You'd better get out and let me and Win rep for you. We'll tally them cows with the stole calves."

"I'm growing used to fear by now," she said with a tight smile. "Yesterday and the day before, I think I would have agreed. But all they do is yell and rage, and I am finding that words aren't the same as violence."

"Women or not, you're in danger of violence. You are plain hated here."

"I'll risk it. The young women will too. No one will harm pregnant women. And I am seeing things, things that perhaps you've not noticed. For instance, Hamilton Bark is not here and hasn't been since the beginning. And neither is that red-headed Lorenzo Strunck."

Dang, she was right.

"The calves are somewhere, and the remaining Hook bulls are also somewhere — probably dead. Sam's tally records show forty-five. But none have shown up here. I think there are crews out away from here killing longhorn bulls and herding the Fishhook calves someplace. I think there is another crew guarding the calves. They are newly weaned and would bolt away to find their mothers if they were not carefully guarded. I also fear that Lorenzo Strunck is on a manhunt, and Padlock and Jerome are the ones he's hunting for."

I figgered she was right. She was plumb smart. Smarter than me.

"Maybe I'll ask Win to get on out and try to

link up with them Injuns and maybe hunt down them calves and look for dead longhorn bulls and all. I brought some extra cuffs and a shotgun I'll lend him. I'll stay here and look after you women and help tally."

"He's been good to us here," said Maud.

"I'll take over here. The buckaroos may not respect me much, Mrs. Hook, but they will respect the star."

"I watched you deal with those stockmen, Mr. Oglesby. They respect you, whether or not they show it."

That felt plumb good. "Ma'am, it'd be easier if you women sort of stuck close to this sheepwagon here."

"No. I will move about. I want them to see a widow in black. I want them to see Mrs. Sam Hook. I want them to — every time they see me, Mr. Oglesby — to remember that night."

"That's what I'm afraid of," I replied quietly.

It settled into a rare May evening. The cattle were bawling. The mamas wanting to pair up with the new-weaned calves; the steer calves sore and sniffing their behinds; the drovers hunkered around the cookfires sopping up sowbelly and beans. The women cooked on that rinkydink cookstove in the sheepwagon. I ate there, and Win did too. He kept his bedroll close to the wagon, and the Hook draft horse staked nearby.

"Win," I said, "I'd like you to ride out tonight and see if you can hook up with the Injuns to the Big Belts. I'd like you to do it when it's black as pitch and not be seen. I figger your old boss Ham Bark, and that hardcase Strunck, and a few like that are out prowling. I want to find that herd of weaned Hook calves. I want to locate the bulls, dead or alive. I figger they're all shot, but we need to see it for evidence. And I want you to guard the bucks and let them know they're in bad trouble."

He nodded. "And you'll look after the women."

"Sure will."

"Constance's about ready. I'd like to be here for that."

I grinned. "I'm sure you would, you being the pappy."

"I — aw, hell." He grinned, and I could see a mess of teeth in the dark.

"Why didn't you marry her?"

"She wouldn't, is all, Will. She wants city life, not a ranch. Ranching's all I know. She said if I go to San Fransisco with her she'd do it. Well, I won't, but I've been taking care of her. If she has the kid while I'm gone, you take care of her, hear?"

"I hear. What's the name gonna be?"

227

"Maud. Maud says there have been twenty-three Mauds born in White Sulphur."

"How about a boy?"

He hesitated. "Maybe Wilbur."

"Nicest thing ever happened to me," I said.

I slid him the shotgun and two of my three pairs of cuffs, and he got his horse saddled up. Along about eleven or so, with all them buckaroos snoring, he vanished. By dawn he'd be well up into the Big Belts hunting Blackfeet and stolen calves and maybe a few dead bulls.

I like to sleep comfortable, so I dragged out the camp cot and mattress I brought along in the buggy, and the bedroll and tent. I got all set up next to Maud's wagon and turned in. I'm one to get a sore throat if I sleep in the open, even on a mild night, so I do it my way and stay snug. I laid the six-gun up by my pillow, pulled my boots off, and got all snugged down.

The middle of the night I woke up to the dangdest clatter. Then there was a hellacious crash, and I heard them women screaming and weeping. I peered out of my tent and grabbed my shooter. There was the sheepwagon on its side, the up-wheels spinning slow in the starlight, and the women crawling out in their flannel nightshirts. And five, six bronco billies standing there grinning mean.

I bolted out of my tent barefoot in my red

longies, trapdoor down, too, but I didn't care none. "Hold it!" I yelled. "Don't move or I'll shoot."

They just stood there all in a slouch. "Worse is coming if these women don't get out right now," snarled one of the black shapes.

"Mister," I said, "raise your paws. There's four of you and I got six shots and I shoot pretty good. You stand real still."

They did that, hands up.

"Maud? You all right? The ladies all right?"

The three had crawled out and were standing up now.

"No, we're not all right," she replied tartly. "We're bruised and Caroline's hand was crushed when the stove fell on it, and I suspect that Constance —"

The girl was crying.

"All right. You four, you set the wagon right. You get those wheels on the ground."

One of them drovers yawned. "Fatso's all wind. Let's go hit the hay."

He started off in the dark, and I wasn't gonna let that happen so I winged him in the arm. He howled and run off but them others froze. I heard shouts from all over, as the camp woke up.

"Right that wagon," I snarled. "Next time I shoot for your lights."

They did, rocking and hauling until they got it up.

"Now get in there and straighten it up."

"I rather they didn't," snapped Maud.

"You!" I barked at one. "Get in there and lift that stove back and plug in the stovepipe."

He did and I kept them others covered while he worked. Pretty soon he came out, just as Dan Monk barreled up.

"You get out of here now," I told them. "Monk, I'm holding you responsible. Any more trouble and I'm making arrests."

He yawned. "Arrest yourself," he said. "If those women aren't gone by dawn, and you too, fatso, it's your funeral."

They wandered off.

I pulled the empty from my six-gun and slipped in fresh. I don't know about others, but I always keep six rounds in.

"Thank you once again, Mr. Oglesby," said Maud.

I seen a lamp flare up in there and moving shadows on the wagon canvas, and then someone blew out the lights. But I could hear Caroline, the one with the bruised hand, sniffling in there.

I figgered that was it for the night, so I crawled back into my tent and fell asleep in two seconds.

I was awakened at dawn.

"Oglesby, come out of there with your hands up. If you touch iron, you're dead."

I peered out and there were all them stockmen: Stapp, Monk, Stope, Jung, Fiske, and all, plus half a dozen mean-looking hands, and every one had an iron pointed at me. I eased out slow.

One of them buckaroos kicked the tent away and lifted my six-gun. I seen Maud peering out of the sheepwagon door.

"Get dressed," Monk snapped.

I did, fast as I could.

"Harness that Hook horse to the sheepwagon. You and the women are taking a ride."

I got the big draft horse off his picket, dropped on the collar and hames and breastband and all, and got him buckled in.

"Get up there and take the reins," Monk continued. "Where's Coop? He's going too."

"I don't know."

"Oglesby, you're being escorted down to Livingston and the Northern Pacific. I'm sending along three men who don't give a damn who or what they shoot – men, women, or sheriffs. You try anything and those women and you are dead. They are going to put you in the first train that comes, east or west, it makes never no mind. If those women show up in

231

these parts again they'll get horsewhipped to pulp. If Maud Wall causes trouble about the Hook place, she'll beg to die before we're done with her. And you, fatso — you show up here again and you're dead, sheriff or no sheriff. You just resigned."

He grinned. The long sun made his eyes glint.

Maud Hook spoke quietly from the wagon. "A young lady is in labor. You will please wait until she's delivered. A bouncing wagon is no place —"

"Like hell we'll wait. That's her tough luck," Monk yelled. "Let her have the bastard in a bouncing sheepwagon."

Maud paled. "I'd like a bucket of water and kindling if you please." She glared at Monk with them cat-eyes and danged if she didn't back him down.

"Get her the stuff," he snarled at one of his toughs.

I figgered if Maud could back him off, maybe I could.

"How are you going to put people on a train and keep them there? At gunpoint? The conductor would stop it in two seconds."

Monk grinned. "It isn't a passenger train you're getting on. They'll lock you in a boxcar. Now get rolling. You try anything, Oglesby, and you all are dead."

I wheeled the wagon south. Those three toughs looked mean and ready to do anything. I heard a moan about every five minutes I figgered.

"Maud," I whispered quiet, "don't stick your head out, but tell me. How's the lady doing?"

Maud sighed. "It's normal now. But when the time comes we'll need to stop. Especially if there are problems. I'll need . . . I don't know what I'll need."

"I'll just stop. Let 'em howl. There any weapons in there? Hook leave a revolver or anything?"

"No, nothing."

"Hide what you can in your skirts," I said. "Food, knife, anything to pry a boxcar door. Water flask. Get yourselves fixed."

"I have a baby to deliver. And I don't think they'll do what he said. They'll just leave us at Livingston."

"Maud, dang it," I hissed, "you're a witness to a lynching and a lot of theft."

She was silent. "If you insist," she whispered at last.

I concentrated on the road, steering around spring potholes so's to keep Constance from being jarred. Not that it made much difference now.

One of the three toughs was out front a hundred yards. The other two flanked me but behind, out of my sight.

It sure was a pretty drive down the Shields with the Crazy Mountains, jagged peaks, rearing up on my left and the Bridgers on my right. Livingston was a division point on the NP, down where the Yellowstone turns south toward the geysers. If they were going to shut them women in a boxcar, Livingston was sure the place to do it, all right.

The moaning was coming faster now, every couple of minutes. Pretty soon Maud stuck her head out and said it was time to stop − if they'd let us.

I whoaed up that big gray. "Gimme that cast-iron fry pan quick," I whispered, "in case I have to brain someone."

The two flankers rode up, ornery.

"Get moving, Oglesby," said one.

"Can't. Baby's coming now. They need quiet and some hot water without it slopping all over and −"

"Get moving," muttered the one with no front teeth.

"You're talking to the law. And we're stopping for now."

He leered. "We ain't even in Meagher County, fatso. You get moving and if they don't like it, too bad."

The other one had a hand on his shooter. "We'll have this baby and then go."

Several things happened so fast I hardly could figger it. The one with no teeth, he swung off his sorrel and up beside me. I knocked him cold with the fry pan, and he slid off and landed in the grass, in a heap. Then the other yelled at me and I seen he had his shooter out. "Hands up, Oglesby. Drop it."

I dropped the pan. And I heard Caroline's bawling in there.

"Get down," said the other as the third one loped back.

I did.

"The sheriff brained Tracy," said the remaining flanker. "Tie the Sheriff up. We've leaving him here."

The point man pulled some piggin string from his possibles, lashed my hands behind my back so tight the blood wasn't running, and then did the same to my calves. The one I brained was coming to, groaning.

"Lucky for you he's not dead, fatso. If he was, you would be."

They tied on their horses and drove off. I watched that wagon get smaller and smaller along the road. I thought of them women inside, trying to bring a baby into the world in that bouncing rig. And finally I realized I was alone, trussed up hand and foot in the middle of nowhere, halfway between the roundup camp and Livingston.

It was quiet. The grasses were tall and waving in the breeze. The sun was warm. A fat rattler was sunning himself on a tan rock ten feet away, watching me warily.

And I wasn't going nowhere.

CHAPTER 17

It sure was quiet. I was maybe sixteen, eighteen miles from the roundup camp and my gear. And maybe thirty yards from the Shields River. And only ten feet from a rattler.

I had a jackknife in my pocket but my hands were tied behind my back and I couldn't get at it. The thong bit so hard my fingers prickled.

The river looked like the best bet. Maybe I could soak the thong and loosen it up. I dragged myself down a bit by kicking my feet and humping. I kept an eye on that rattler but I was plumb helpless if it got any notions.

I worked along, tossing my legs and dragging my butt, and by the time I had got twenty yards I'd worked up a sweat and my heart was hammering. I dripped along, wondering if I could roll since it was a downslope. But a patch of prickly pear cured me of that notion. After a half hour of kicking and butt-scraping I made fifty more yards. I was miserable and getting parched.

There wasn't a rock or nothing I could use at

that thong so I kept thumping down until I was tuckered out. Then I rolled onto my side and panted for a while until I could try it again. I was about as hot and sticky as a man gets, and the suit was a mess of grass stains and dirt. A bolting rabbit scared tarnation out of me. Anything with fangs could have had a free feed off of me. I was getting desperately tired and I wished I had kept myself in better shape.

The thongs were tight as ever and I began to fear I'd lose my feet and hands if I didn't get blood into them soon. It took another hour to get to the Shields, and when I finally got there I seen my problems were just beginning. The stream was running between cutbanks and the edges were choked with brush. If I fell over the edge, I'd drown for sure, trussed up the way I was. And I didn't know how to get through the brush and down to water. Some big snake slithered away, scaring me bad, but it didn't have rattles.

I had to go sideways along the bank and find a place where I could get to water, so I swung left and humped and kicked along. At least it was a little cooler in that tall grass and brush. Finally, when I was just about at the end of my string I seen a little game trail going down, and twisted myself into it. It was about right for rabbits and foxes, but not for one big sheriff.

There was hardly room to kick so I had to dig my toes into the moist clay and sort of squeeze out a few inches at a time. The twigs whipped my face every time I skinched ahead. It took another half hour, seems like, to wiggle down to water's edge. When I finally got there I lay panting a bit and trying to figger the next step. The river was running swift and one false step would drown me. I finally squirmed on down and got my boots into the water, and then my bound-up calves. It was cold! That water was snowmelt right off the peaks. It felt good for a minute but it was soon numbing my legs. I began kicking and straining that wet throng but it didn't do nothing, just stayed tight. But it seemed like more blood was getting to my feet and they tingled a little. There was a sharp-edged rock right near the bank and I stared longingly at it, but I didn't see no way to get there on my back in that rapid water. So I lay there, feet freezing, top half sweating, and heart pounding, trying to figger what next. I was getting mad.

That sharp rock was about the only choice. I had to get my hands to it some way, and get a drink too — I was so parched I was feeling faint. So I kicked my feet up onto dry land, and rolled over onto my gut, almost going too far and into the current, which scared me bad.

Then I scissored myself until I got my head in and a noseful of water. But I drank like a camel. A danged wave splashed over my face and half drowned me. I got a windpipe full of water and coughed. That cool icewater sure felt good for a moment, so I rested and stared at the vast clean sky.

Then came the worst part. I had to slide into the current on my back and hold myself in place with my legs on the bank. I had to get my hands over the sharp rock and saw. I began inching down, and pretty soon my hands and the thong were in the water and the thong started to soak. My whole body ached but I kept whipping my arms and twisting, trying to loosen that thong. It held tight. I inched out more and took more water down my windpipe. The current was tugging now and I was close to losing my hold on dry ground.

Now, instead of feeling hot I was half freezing to death. And I had gone in so far there was no way I could lever myself back up to dry land. The clay was slippery up there and my legs had no purchase. I was weak as a pup and figgered I had maybe fifteen minutes before I turned too numb to move.

I seen something shiny on the bottom and it was my jackknife, which had slid out of my pocket with my legs high like that. I hunched on over until I was on top of the knife and began feeling around with my tied-up hands. The water was rushing over me and splashing up my nose. I kept feeling around – the thongs were a little looser now – until my fingers touched metal. The trouble was, I couldn't open the knife or saw with it.

That thong was loosened a little and I kept working at it. Pretty soon I was able to get a thumbnail into the blade and pull. It opened a little and finally snapped out. Oh, that was a moment to rejoice. And then my numb hands lost it. My arms and hands and fingers had turned so aching cold that I didn't have no feel, and the knife was gone. I thrashed around a lot but it was plumb gone. There was nothing to do now but yank and yank on that piggin string and hope the wet would loosen it. Another of them waves slapped me. I was getting desperate and crazy, and thrashing around like a madman. I roared and yanked and snarled at the thong – and felt something give. Not a snap, but sort of an oozing apart. I elbowed and yanked with the last energy in me and that thong parted and my hands were free. About time, too. I was half-dead. I rolled over and spotted the knife about a yard downstream, glittering in the muddy water. I got it, cut my leg thongs, crawled on up to dry grass, and cried.

I ain't much of a man. Men don't cry. But I was so glad to be alive and have the sun warming my bones that I wept. Finally, I got out of my wet suit, wrung the water from it, and spread it out on the grass. I poured water out of my boots and then just lay there in my wet longies letting the sun and the zephyrs dry me while I got some strength back. It was an hour before I even felt like moving. The sun was still high, it being late May. I was starved but didn't pay it any heed.

I thought to head north to the roundup camp and my buggy and food. I could get there in six hours or so if I could walk steadily. Livingston was maybe thirty miles the other way, and feeling the way I did I knew I couldn't make it. I wasn't sure I could even get back to camp. I'd just forget about the women. There wasn't nothing I could do anyway — them ladies would be long gone in some boxcar.

With Maud gone, it'd be all over. I figgered the bucks would vanish and there'd be peace in the Smith River valley just like before.

The sun was still buttering warmth on me and I quit shivering. The black worsted was steaming and even my red longies were getting warm, wet as they were. The big sky never looked so good to me. I rolled over in the tall grass and let the sun warm my backside while I dozed.

I'd had enough sheriffing to last me a lifetime. Maybe them hardcases were right when they told me I'd resigned and was leaving the county. Dang, I hated to have them talk to me like that, like I wasn't anybody to contend with. I had gotten feisty with them at the roundup camp and all it got me was a wagon ride and a brush with death.

I wished I'd never met Sam Hook. He had gotten me into this even if he was weeks dead now. I couldn't shake that feller. It wasn't his ghost or spirit; it was just the memory of him and them eyes boring into me.

I got up and turned the black suit and pants over to let the other side fry. They were tolerably clean because the river had washed the grit and sweat and stain out.

It got along to five or six and the heat was still pouring in. I began to feel pretty good except for my belly, so I got dressed and stood there in that vast, lonely valley with the most beautiful mountains in the world, the Crazies, to the east, the blue Bridgers to the west, and peaceful ranching country in between.

"Love Maud," I muttered and started south. If I could hold up for thirty miles I might make it to Livingston around dawn. Always assuming

I didn't get lost in the night. I wondered some how the birthing had gone and whether that Constance was fine and whether there was a new Wilbur or a new Maud in the world.

My boots were squishy but I made pretty good time. I walked for what I figgered was a half hour at a time and then rested. Some long slopes were bad and I didn't know whether a worn-out heavyweight like me could manage them. I had to stop even on low grades and catch my wind. But I kept on and turned the walking into kind of a rhythm. It was turning cool too fast, but my clothes were dry enough to warm me. I wished a wagon or a rider — anyone — would come along, but none did. I was alone and there was no help anywhere.

Along about ten or eleven, with some last light still bluing the mountains, I got awful tired and my feet were blistering up. So I rested good and got a drink from the river. I had to ford a couple of creeks that came down from the Crazies which got my boots all sloshy again. My gut was howling, but I just said, Wilbur, you're gonna do it or die trying. And I did it. I vowed that if I ever got back to White Sulphur I was going to shed some weight and get into shape again.

Montana nights are delightsome and I got to enjoying the soft air. Maybe toward the dawn it'd be nippy. My left foot was getting rubbed raw, so I slid that stubborn wet boot off and cut a slit in it with my knife to loosen it up. It helped. I was down to fifteen-minute walks between rests but I kept on pushing. During the rests I learned to curl up in the grass and snooze a minute. There was scarcely a moon, but my eyes were used to the night by then and I could make out the ruts of the road.

I hoped them women took my advice and packed a little food and gear before getting stuck into a noisy, cold boxcar. Then they'd have a little something. It could be days, even a week, before anyone opened up that car. That infant was getting a pretty rough start in life, and so was its mother. Win told me she was from Martinsdale, a storekeeper's daughter.

I sure didn't know why I was doing this. Miss Gillian, the schoolmarm back at White Sulphur, looked up Rubicon for me after Francis Harp told me I'd crossed it. She said that a long time ago. If Julius Caesar had failed, after he crossed it with his legions and defied the senate, he'd be dead. It was do or die, the Rubicon was. I figgered that was about right, and old Harp had a way with words. Do or die.

I was so tuckered I didn't make time like I should and I hobbled along sore as a bad tooth. It was dawn when I finally limped into the

Yellowstone valley, and the sun was lighting the peaks when I stumbled to the rails, and it was an hour later that I marched my bloody stumps into the NP station and asked the telegraph operator where to find the stationmaster.

He looked me over pretty tart and his waxed mustache tips quivered. But he pointed at a stair that had a big No Admittance sign above it. I went on up.

The stationmaster was a fellow with eyes that were just meant for chasing hoboes. But I showed him my star and I still had some soggy papers in my breast pocket to prove that I was who I said I was. I told him what I knew: that three women with an hours-old infant had got stuck on a boxcar by some abductors sometime after ten at night, that they had been shanghied or kidnapped and driven there in a sheepwagon.

"That wagon's here," interrupted the master. "Yard superintendent reported it. We pulled it over yonder." He pointed out that second-story window. "No horse, though." A certain gentleness filled his eyes as he looked me over. "My name's Tecumseh Branson, Sheriff. Why don't you just sit down while I go over last night's sheet." He found a manifest and studied it some. "Westbound most likely. Left here at nine minutes to two. Laid over in Bozeman to let the eastbound highball pass. Should be nearing Butte."

"Any eastbound they could be on?"

"An eastbound got in two hours later, around four. But that was passenger."

"Could you wire Butte, have them stop it and search the cars?"

He trotted down to the telegraph man and I gimped down after. They composed a message and like lightning that fellow was *ditting* and *datting* on the key like some magic. I never figgered how anyone could do that so fast.

"I told them to hold the freight and have a look, and to await further instructions from you, Sheriff, if those women show up," Branson said.

"Nothing to do but wait," I said.

"You look done in. Would you like some chow?"

"I'm so starved I could eat my own left arm."

"The Northern Pacific will be glad to feed a starving sheriff," Branson said. "And we'll give those ladies passes for the next eastbound coach." He smiled amiably. "There's a couch in my office there. Maybe you'd like to take a snooze."

I hit that couch like a load of bricks and was out cold when they brought in some breakfast.

They had a time reviving me, but after they did I piled into flapjacks and drank a quart of coffee and then settled into that sofa again.

"Mr. Branson," I said as I settled in, "maybe you'd better get the Park County sheriff over here, if you would. Bo Svee in his name. I can give him an accounting and description of them hardcases if they're still in town. And I'll want to borrow a draft horse from him to take that wagon back where it came from."

"You rest, Sheriff. You're as exhausted as a man can get and still live, I think. I'll send for the sheriff a little later. I don't know how you got yourself untied at the river and I don't know how you walked thirty miles, but you did it, and not many men could or would."

That sure made me feel lightsome, and then I fell asleep again. But in no time at all someone was shaking and rattling me. I didn't want to open one eye, much less two.

It was that telegraph operator with the waxed mustache and a garter on his sleeve and hair parted down the middle of his skull. He handed me a yellow sheet with his penciled transcription on it:

WOMEN FOUND ON WESTBOUND 27 SAFE WITH MALE INFANT STOP AT EL MUNDO HOTEL NOW AND

Dang, that was good.

"Thank you," I said. "I'm needing some shuteye now, but I'd like to be awakened at two this afternoon. Need to talk with your sheriff."

"We'll roust you out, Mr. Oglesby. Glad it turned out good."

I was out again and don't remember nothing of that day. At five o'clock when the station-master was about to fold up for the day, they shook me awake. I seen my shirt and suitcoat had been cleaned and pressed, and I thanked them all.

Bo Svee was sitting there too, a big black-haired one-eyed man. He'd lost an eye trying to stop a saloon fight between a fireman and banty brakeman. The banty shoved a broken bottle into Svee's face.

"Hello, Will. At last we meet, eh? I got you a horse for that wagon and no need to return it. We found the gray that pulled it down, aban-doned out of town. Some hike you had."

He was sitting there admiring me; I didn't figger I done anything to deserve his admira-tion, but it felt nice. Pretty soon I was telling him the whole thing: Sam Hook, the stockmen, the lynching, Jeff Bark and Clyde Park, Maud and the Injuns, and all.

"Get Strunck," he said. "I've got flyers on him coming out the kazoo. You need iron? I lifted an old shooter off a drunk cowboy a while ago and he never came to fetch it. Let's get a steak on Park County, hoss. And we'll walk over to my office and I'll give you that iron for your empty leather."

That was about the best slab of beef I ever put teeth to, and before we were done eating and sucking sourmash at the Iron Horse Saloon we were fast friends, Sheriff Svee and me.

Afterward he fetched the iron and then I hobbled over with him to look at the sheep-wagon. It looked sound enough. Then we waited for the eastbound, which came chuffing in a bit early.

Maud was the first off and Caroline followed.

"Where's Constance? Where's the baby?"

"In Butte," she replied wearily. "I insisted she stay in the hotel with the baby for two or three days, and have a doctor in attendance."

"You and the young lady are looking perky, Maud. This here is Sheriff Bo Svee of Park County. This here is Maud Hook and Caroline . . . uh . . . Caroline."

We took them women on over to the NP Hotel. I figgered to get started north in the morning, but I wondered whether to hold over for Constance.

"We won't be seeing Constance," Maud explained. "She's going on to San Francisco. There's nothing left here for her, you see. They kindly allowed me to draft a check. . . ."

"I ain't gonna see little Wilbur?" I grinned at Svee. "My namesake."

"You the pappy?" asked Svee.

"Wish I was," I replied.

Maud arched an eyebrow.

There was a room for me, too, at the NP, and I slept like a dead man.

CHAPTER 18

Next morning me and the women set out on the two-day trip to the Sixteen country in that rattly sheepwagon. Svee's horse was a strong one and I figgered to make good time. I was plenty worried about running into them hardcases, but the roundup would be over and maybe they'd be gone. Even so, we'd probably run into the drovers pushing the sale herd down to the NP pens at Livingston.

Maud told me what had happened. The toughs wouldn't stop so Constance had her baby in the bouncing and jolting wagon, with Maud holding her hand. It went pretty fast, maybe even faster than if they had stopped. But it had been hard to clean up or boil water with it sloshing around. All that happened seven or eight hours before they were forced into a boxcar, so Constance got a rest.

They got to the rails late at night. The hardcases held the women beside the tracks until just before the westbound pulled out, then threw them into a car with lots of crates in it and rolled that door shut just as the car jolted into movement. It was so black in there that they could only feel their way around, but they got Constance and that infant stretched out and they all huddled close in the blackness for warmth until they were freed over to Butte. They were treated right kindly by the NP folks there and the local constable, put in a hotel and given return passes and all.

"And now you're riding back into trouble," I said.

Maud, on the seat beside me, just stared off into the Crazy Mountains, and said, "I can't quit now."

"You scared?"

"I've never stopped being scared since the night they lynched Sam."

We drove along quiet, stopping now and then to let that draft horse water and rest. Me and Maud were silent as a graveyard, but Miss Caroline back there was perky and began chattering. It turned out she was the daughter of some gambler and faro table operator up at Fort Benton. He had a run of rotten luck and when he hit empties with three dudes at his table, he made one final bet: a night with his daughter for each of them against all he had lost. He lost again, and that's how come she ended up with Maud. It sounded like one sad tale, but the way she told it, she had a roaring good time for three nights. Maud blushed.

Along about suppertime I made out a big herd of beeves ahead. It was just as I feared. Drovers were pushing the market beeves down to the NP after the roundup. And me with two women and one cowboy gun and no spare rounds. There was nothing for it but to drive ahead and hope for the best.

That mess of cattle was bawling and lowing along the Shields River, and I seen plenty of longhorns mixed in. Maud seen them too.

"I'm counting," she said. "Forty-one so far."

They had set up night-camp and were cooking beans when we drove in. This bunch was smiling drovers, not hardcases and toughs, and I was mighty glad of that. The ramrod was potbellied Elmer Marshall of the Stope and Jung outfit.

"Looks like we'll be parking here for the night, Elmer," I said.

"Suit yourself. There's beans boiling."

"I got a question or two, Elmer. We seen forty, fifty Hook longhorns in this herd. Was the sale of them authorized by the Hook Partners, them Injuns?"

Marshall shook his head. "Those be Association beeves, signed for by Ham Bark. That's forfeit beef because the Fishhook didn't send drovers to the gather. The district always does that so that each ranch carries its weight. Each outfit sends three, four hands."

"I've counted forty-six steers," said Maud.

"Fifty Hook steers, ma'am."

"How much is the market price of my steers, Mr. Marshall?"

"Oh, twenty-six, twenty-eight dollars."

"And what are the drovers earning?"

"Forty and found, most of them."

"Per month. And if the Fishhook had sent four hands for the six days of roundup, how much wage would that have totaled?"

"About a month, ma'am. I know what you're driving at."

"I'm driving at the obvious fact that two steers, three at the most, would have compensated. Don't forget that Win Coop was there, working hard."

Marshall looked uncomfortable and scratched his behind.

"I'd like to see the shipping papers, Elmer," I said.

I checked through. There was a tally by brand, signed by each owner or his rep and a sale authorization signed by each owner or his rep. The Hook steers were signed for by Ham Bark, the district president.

"I'm thinking, Elmer, Mrs. Hook has overpaid a little. By about forty-seven beeves. I think you and them boys, you'd better cut out forty-seven Hook steers before it gets dark, and we'll let you take three to market for the grazing district."

Marshall looked puzzled. "Can't do it. I have my orders and I'd get us all poleaxed by our employers. And you ain't got the authority."

"I have sheriff authority. And I'll be taking you in on theft charges, rustling charges," I roared.

"You figure we're rustling?"

"I figger that Mrs. Hook's being stolen blind and as sure as I'm sheriff I'm gonna stop it."

All the drovers were staring at me now.

"What am I gonna tell those—"

"I'm writing you a receipt and a sheriff order right now. And Maud here will sign a release for the three beeves she's paying the district."

That did it. He stalked over to them others and they slowly saddled up, not liking it because they thought they were done for the day. Then they began cutting the longhorns out. It's never easy cutting stock, especially with no pens around, but them big horns sticking out above the dark mass of Herefords sure helped. Pretty soon they had their forty-seven and had driven them a mile north and turned them loose along the river.

Later, Elmer came on over to me. "Those hands each want a sheriff order signed by you to show back at their outfit."

That seemed reasonable. I didn't want no one fired for doing an honest act. So I wrote out six orders: "47 Fishhook steers removed from sale herd by order of Meagher County Sheriff," and I signed each one. The buckaroos tucked the sheets into their possibles and I seen a smile or two. I don't think they liked the theft neither.

"Thank you," said Maud. "I don't know what I would do without you, Wilbur."

But it worried me plenty. It was one more thing the leading lights and county officials would hang me with. I was in too deep now to back out.

When I turned down the Sixteen Mile road the next afternoon I seen something off in the hills to the north I didn't want to see — a column of carrion birds wheeling. Just about every kind, I figgered, from magpies to crows to vultures. I drove as close as I could and stopped.

"Maud, I've got to have a look over there. We're maybe two miles from the Fishhook. You keep a sharp eye and if you see anyone coming, you whip this nag and get into the house and bar the door. Don't wait for me."

She nodded and I clambered down and started up the long slope. My feet were still a pair of bloody stumps.

After a few hundred yards through silvery sage the death-smell began to reach me. When I finally eased over a low ridge lined with ponderosa and stared into a hollow, I seen what it was. About thirty-five longhorn bulls, long dead, and mostly ate up by coyotes and wolves and foxes and a whole skyful of black birds. I scanned the trees around there looking for trouble but I didn't see nothing. So I stood on that crest and yelled, and that whole flapping black bunch lifted off with a raucous howl.

I pulled my handkerchief over my nose but it didn't do no good. It was a sickly smell and made my gut heave. I was about to get out of there when something else — some color off in a draw on the left — caught my eye. I forced myself to walk over there and it was bad . . . I was sick.

Lying there was what was left of Jerome Padlock, with a black bullethole through his shirt. The eyes were gone and the flesh was tore away; not much left. I felt my stomach lurching and I got down on all fours expecting to lose lunch. My eyes got watered up but I didn't lose lunch, and pretty soon I swallowed down the bile in my throat and stood up again. There wasn't any burying to do. Later maybe someone could pick up the bones.

I tried to figger what had happened. It looked like they had gathered the Hook bulls and drove them here, close to the Fishhook Ranch, and shot them. Then they left someone around to ambush the Injuns when they came to see what was dead and drawing carrion-eaters. Well, they got one. I circled upwind – I couldn't manage walking downstream from that sickening pile of guts – and I found a place maybe fifty yards away, well hidden by boulders and pines, where there were some boot prints and stomped grass. They had set a trap and got Jerome. I wondered if old Padlock had bought it too, but I didn't see nothing. I had the evidence I needed – the bootprints at an ambush place – so I hightailed down to the road, still green around the gills.

Maud looked at me sharp and kept quiet. I got that nag trotting and we were close to the Fishhook before I felt like saying anything.

"The bulls," I muttered. "All the rest, or nearly. Shot a week or so ago."

She just pursed her lips and looked grim, and Miss Caroline looked quivery.

"That ain't all."

"Oh no . . ."

"Jerome."

"Oh, Will." She clung to me and buried her face in my arm for a long while.

"Too far gone to pick up, Maud. They shot him from ambush. It don't look good for you or Padlock, if he's still alive."

She couldn't say anything and sat mute the rest of the way in.

When we got there I figgered it was pretty safe, but you never know, so I looked over that dark place sharp. There was no fire; only a desolate silence at Sam Hook's ranch.

"I figger you're safe here, Maud. They think you've gone to Keokuk or Pocatello or Alaska by now, so they don't have any reason to come hunting you here."

I let them off at the verandah and had a quick look-see of the house, then drove the sheepwagon right into the barn where no one would spot it. I took good care of that nag of Svee's and walked on over to Sam Hook's house.

"Maud, I don't want no one knowing you're here, so no lamps at night; cook as little as possible, only at night or before dawn. No fireplace fires if you can manage without. And move about after dark if you can."

She nodded and I seen a flash of that cat-eye look in her face.

"You ever shoot a gun?"

"No – but I watched – that night."

"I'm going to load these guns," I said. "If you're in trouble, bar the doors and shoot from various loops. Never the same loophole twice. It doesn't matter if you can't aim; just make noise."

"I will make a great noise, Mr. Oglesby."

"Caroline, you shoot, too. Just get the butt into your shoulder or you'll feel it."

"I'm a good shot, Mr. Oglesby. I have demolished a thousand airtights and whiskey bottles."

"Good. Just don't shoot me or Win or Padlock."

Maud smiled.

I stopped long enough to wolf down some canned peaches and grab Hook's hunting rifle and some shells, then I eased out to the horse pasture above the barn to find a bronc. After walking my sore dogs off I finally got a rope over one and bridled and saddled him. He crowhopped and sunfished so bad I thought one fat sheriff was going to hit the dirt like a cannonball and never rise again, but he settled down and I took off into the night.

I ain't much of a saddleman and I knew I was going to be sore as a dental appointment, but there wasn't much time and I had no choice. I didn't know where I was going exactly or what I was hunting for, but I figgered Widow

261

Thwait's abandoned house and pens would be the place to start. I wasn't much for cutting over foothills. I'd get lost easy, Big Dipper or not, so I just set out on the roads and on up the Smith River valley. Maybe them heroes in Ned Buntline dime novels could thread the needle in the middle of the night but I sure couldn't. I was just a big-gut two-hundred-sixty-pound sheriff who stuck to roads and used buggies.

Some time around two or three I hit the Deep Creek road. At least I thought it was — the silver moon was no help. But the time was about right. I was chilled and sore and cussing myself because I didn't bring chow or a bedroll or anything else. Just that bolt-action rifle, shells, and that shooter on my hip.

I turned west toward the Thwait place. Along about four or five — close to dawn that time of year — I knew I was close because I was hearing something on the night breeze, the bawling of calves. Them newly-weaned calves don't quit bawling for their mammies for days after they are weaned. Even now, a week or so later, they were still taking turns blatting into the night. It all made sense: the best way to wean a bunch of calves is in a pen somewhere, and what better place than the abandoned Thwait property. Her stock had been auctioned and them hands, Kid Dunham and Len

Carroll, were long gone.

I stopped the bronc to think a little. He didn't like thinking and stamped his foot and lashed his tail. He was a mad horse. That is one reason I don't ride saddle much. The nags are always mad at me because of my weight. They lay back their ears and give me grumpy looks. This one had been looking for a shot at me all night.

What I was wondering was whether the place was guarded; whether there was a night rider out; and who all might be there. And beyond that, what I'd do about it.

I decided what I'd do first is make sure it was the missing longhorn calves. And try to figger out how many hardcases were in the house or around the place. And who. And then I'd pull back and try to hook up with Padlock and Win and figger something out.

I supposed they'd have a night watch. They weren't dumb and they would need to guard against Padlock. On the other hand, they would figger that me and the women were gone and maybe relax. . . .

I rode up close as I dared and slid off that nag in a little sagebrush draw. I was about to tie him up when that sumbitch sunk his teeth into my sore behind, and I snarled and kicked him good in the belly — which made some noise. I hoped the bawling calves covered it up. That dang Sam Hook didn't break his broncs good at all.

I puffed out of that draw and eased through the dark to the pens. There was a murky mass of young stuff in there but I couldn't tell much. Longhorns come every color in the book and this bunch looked lighter-hued than Herefords would but I couldn't swear to it.

I got bolder and decided to have a look at the calves. My black worsted suit was like an inkspot at midnight so I figgered I was pretty safe, especially with them calves making a racket.

Dang, I couldn't find the broncs. The next pen was full of calves and so was the third pen. This was one big-time deal — maybe eight hundred or a thousand of the little buggers. Maybe the whole Hook calf crop.

I still wanted a count on the broncs so I prowled closer to the Thwait house. The horses were right there in the yard where Mary Ellen had blown a magpie to bits. Eight of them, milling around because they got wind of me. Maybe eight men, then, unless one or two horses were spares.

Next thing, my head exploded. I started to fall and the last thing I seen, that jasper with no front teeth was hulked above me.

CHAPTER 19

Someone was pounding on my skull with a ballpeen hammer. It was daylight but my eyes were so blurred I couldn't make out nothing. I was lying in Widow Thwait's bedroom; I got that straight, but I couldn't figger why some blacksmith was banging on my skull. Then I got it right; no one was. Every pulse of blood was like a mallet.

"Morning, Will."

I focused my eyes some.

"Morning, Hamilton."

"Here's some water."

I sipped and got myself sitting up. There were one or two others there, tough-looking customers.

"Snoops get headaches, don't they. You can't say you weren't warned, over and over, to stay out."

"I seen what I needed to see," I retorted. "The entire Fishhook calf crop."

"You saw a lot of calves, but not Fishhook calves."

265

"I seen the biggest rustling this county's ever had, is what I seen," I replied stubbornly. "And there's a hanging noose for each of you."

Hamilton Bark smiled. "You're mistaken, Will. Each of those calves belongs to the Smith River grazing district. There's not a stockman in the valley who's put his brand to any of them. You go out there and you'll see a rafter lazy eight brand, which is a new one in the Territory. The district will register it in its name."

"I don't give a hoot what brand you burned into them stolen Fishhook calves. You can't cover up rustling with some community brand."

He was getting oranged up, and that meant trouble. "We hoped you wouldn't see it that way, Will. Seeing it that way could be, ah, painful for you."

"I seen what I seen. I seen Fishhook bulls shot in a heap. That's one offense. I seen fifty full-grown Fishhook steers going down the trail to market and your signature on the sheet. That's another offense."

"A perfectly proper assessment against the Fishhook for not supplying drovers."

"Proper, hell."

Bark glared at me. "There's not a rancher in the district that's making a dime off the Hook estate. Those calves are a proper compensation for heavy losses that Hook imposed on us all by letting his common bulls run. We have a right to even things up. What we're doing with these is selling, and with the proceeds we'll buy blooded bulls, the best money can buy. We'll crossfence the district to control breeding better. The district's doing it and no rancher is involved."

"That's just a fancy way of enriching eighteen stockmen," I replied. "That doesn't change it from theft."

My head was worse than ever. Bark looked sour. That tough with no front teeth stared at me from the doorway.

"What's come over you, Will? You used to be a fine fellow, easy to get along with. Now you got thistle up your butt and no one can live with you."

I didn't say anything.

"You've gone crazy trying to be a big-shot sheriff and throwing your weight around. You're too big for your britches. What are you trying to do, anyway? Stop progress? Force all the stockmen to go broke?"

"I swore an oath of office to uphold the law."

"Well, hell, Will, the law got bent a little, but all for a good cause. You know that. And besides, it's all over. It's done, Will. We're about back to the nice quiet valley we had before."

"Done? Nothing's done."

"Will, what's got into you? Maud Wall is somewhere around Portland, Oregon by now. The Blackfeet bucks and Coop all met unfortunate accidents. They're gone. Nobody owns the Fishhook."

My heart sagged down to my toes. The Injuns and Win dead. Jerome I knew about, but Padlock . . . and Win. Maybe Bark was right. It was all over, even if Maud was still around.

"Where's Strunck?" I asked.

"Away on grazing district business."

"Where's away?"

"What's it to you, Oglesby?"

"There's a dozen flyers on him. Did he shoot Jerome Padlock or did you?"

Bark's face flushed orange and then beet red. "There was a felony warrant on that Indian. When he resisted arrest we had to take steps."

"I'll bet you did. From ambush. You or Strunck did it, Ham, and that's murder. I'll be after you for that and a lot more, such as burning down Maud Wall's house."

"Oglesby, you've got a choice. See it our way or show up missing."

"Comes to that, does it? You're fixing to kill a

sheriff to cover it all up?"

"Nothing to cover up, Oglesby. Everything's aboveboard. Peace is at hand. Hook's dead and the three partners are gone. Proper compensation is worked out. You're the last problem we've got."

"You mean the last witness, except maybe Harp."

"Harp's no trouble. We'll hold him down, pry open his jaws, and pour two or three bottles into him, enough so he don't wake up. But you're a problem. I'd hate to see a good sheriff disappear. Think of all the good times ahead for us all. You setting in that office and enjoying life."

"What if I resigned?"

"Resigning's not good enough now." Bark pointed a finger straight at me. "You got two minutes, fatso. You join us and give us no grief, or —"

"Yes?"

"We take you out to that cottonwood there and we prop you up and you disappear."

"So, it does come to that."

"Two minutes, fatso."

The bedroom door slammed and I was almighty alone. My head hurt.

All I had to do was be a potmetal sheriff to enjoy life. Visit Molly. Enjoy all the leading lights of White Sulphur. Play lots of solitaire. Get my teeth around lots of good steaks. Live good and respectable.

Damn you, Sam Hook! Damn you for fixing it that if I live, I'm dead inside, and if I'm dead, I've finally lived. Damn you for calling me mister. Damn you for croaking orders at me from the noose.

What good would the good life be, if I was full of shame and loathing, some potmetal man. What good? Some kind of hell every day. I love life, but here I was chosing between death and death.

I sighed, knowing which way I'd jump. The only bad thing was Maud down there with no one to look after her after I was gone. But I couldn't help her either way, now. If I gave in to Bark, I'd have to chase her to hell and gone.

I fingered the star. I never was worthy of it and now it was paying me back. I ain't manly. I knew I would blubber when they took me out there. But I had no choice now.

The door creaked open and Bark stood there calm.

"You come to your senses?"

I stood up straight. "Just for the record, Hamilton, even if it don't mean anything now, I'm arresting you for murder of Sam Hook, Jerome Padlock, Win Coop, and Padlock. I'm arresting you for rustling calves. I'm arresting you for stealing Fishhook steers. And for burning down Maud's house. And for inciting a lynching. Just for the record, Ham, you and them scummy toughs you've got around you, are under arrest. I'm saying it so you know I died as a sheriff rather than what I was when you and your kind had a thumb on me."

He grinned and nodded. Them two toughs each got an arm and hauled me into the parlor and then out the door. The sun was bright and warm and made me blink, only I couldn't see nothing except the white glare of it because I was too trembly to walk. My face was all wet. I was ashamed to be crying — a poor excuse for a sheriff, I was. I was puke-sick but it didn't matter none.

Then we hit the shade of that lone cottonwood and I seen the silvery sagebrush of the hills, hills that kept on climbing almost to God. It was a desolate place, and that is what turned the widow crazy. They propped me up there and something sagged inside me so bad I could hardly stand, but I forced myself to. I stood up proud and tried to see all them blurred killers. I blinked hard, and blinked again until I cleared my eyes of tears.

Ham was going to do it himself. He wasn't smiling and he wasn't orange mad, neither.

Killing sheriffs ain't everyday business, I figgered. My eyes were leaking again. Them others looked smirky and just stood there, ready to pick up the meat and haul it up to the Big Belts somewhere, and then cave a cutbank over me.

I seen Ham lift his six-gun and that bore come up at me and I whimpered; then Ham got kicked by a mule, and I heard a crack and another crack, and some more, lots of them. Ham's flannel shirt bloomed red, then his face disappeared into pulp, and he dropped that gun and toppled like a tree. And them other two staggered and whirled and fell too.

I couldn't figger what happened except I was alive and they were dead at my feet. I trembled so bad I couldn't think, but I seen Ham's six-gun and I dove for it just as three more toughs boiled from the house. I shot two and some more of them cracks from the hills got the other. One of them thrashed around and started to lift his six-gun at me but another crack from that hillside stopped him cold.

I gaped at it all. Six men dead as mummies. I shook so bad I sat down in the grass and cried. Hell of a sheriff I turned out to be, sobbing like that.

Next thing, there were shadows beside me and an arm around my shoulder and Padlock saying, "It's all over, Sheriff," and Win squatting in front of me and handing me a bandanna, asking if I was okay.

I guessed I was.

Win stood up and I heard him reloading his magazine, and then stalking around there to make sure there were no more surprises.

"Ham said you both was dead."

"Jerome's dead," said Padlock.

"I saw it."

"It's more than I can bear, that young man. Where's Maud?"

"At the Fishhook with the one girl, Caroline."

I stood up and dusted myself off, but I was trembling too bad to walk.

Win returned. "How are the women?" he asked.

"You're a pappy."

He didn't smile none. I told him the whole thing, watched him turn red when I got to the part about birthing in the banging sheepwagon. I got through the NP business, and then I had to tell him: Constance stayed on in Butte . . . and was planning on heading west after that.

Win absorbed all that somberly.

"It was coming," he said. "I only wish I got to see the kid first. But she's okay, she's okay. I got a kid named Wilbur somewheres in this big world. And," he added softly, "some memories of someone I loved."

Padlock and I, we walked away and left Win alone for a bit.

"You fit to travel now, Sheriff?" he asked, some urgency in his voice.

"Are we going somewhere?"

"Back to the Fishhook. Lorenzo Strunck is out in those hills stalking human game. He's been after us. He checks that ranchhouse about once a day."

"Maud!" I scrambled up. "Let's get going. I told them to bar the door and shout anybody shows up, keep banging even if they don't hit nothing. But that Caroline can shoot good."

Win sprang for the pens, opened the gates, and shooed the calves out of each one. The critters spread out onto the spring bunchgrass, or wandered down to the seep for water.

"No one to care for them now. They'd be dead or dying by the time we got back," he said.

We saddled up and bridled a spare because it was going to be a hard six- or seven-hour ride down there. I collected some spare six-guns off of them dead jaspers and doled them out to Win and Padlock.

"Stay spread out in case he starts sniping," I

said. And then we were off, loping, jogging, and walking, making good time without wrecking those broncs. We rode south down the Smith River road but then Padlock led us overland on an angle toward the Fishhook. My head hammered, my butt ached, my thighs were blistered, my feet burned, and my gut was still turning over. But I didn't care. Maud needed us.

Sometime early in the afternoon we topped a rise that gave us our first view into the Sixteen country. Off in the haze I seen the Fishhook Ranch basking in the sun as peaceful as a church.

We rode quiet and spread wide now. Twenty minutes later we topped another long ridge. The place was much closer. I seen one of the women, couldn't tell which, coming from the privy and I was glad of the sight of her. We were gonna be there in time.

But then Win was pointing, and I followed his point and saw that red-headed Lorenzo Strunck watching off a piece. Bad trouble, and us still a mile away, and a downhill mile at that. You can't hurry a bronc down slopes like we faced.

The woman disappeared into the house. We raced down fast, aiming for the next rise. For the moment whatever was happening down there was out of sight. We loped across a long coulee and up, and Win signaled us to dismount as we approached the next ridge. We did, and peered over. It was too far for a six-gun shot, but maybe a carbine would reach.

Strunck was there, gliding toward that house like a big catamount, a lithe giant. He had his revolver out and I knew he'd use it on the women without a second thought.

We left the horses behind that ridge and scrambled down on foot, using some ponderosa copses for cover. I figgered we could alert the women with a shot if we needed to, but that would give us away to Strunck and at that distance we'd never get him.

Strunck slipped around the barn and came dancing at the house.

And then that buffalo gun of Hook's boomed. Why the women used that big Sharps, that fifty-calibre cannon with a kick as would flatten them, I didn't know.

But Strunck sailed six feet backward, smashed by some giant fist, and landed in a heap in the dust.

It was sure quiet.

"Maud," I hollered. "It's Will. Don't shoot. It's Will and Padlock and Win."

There was a stretching silence and then the door opened and she stood there staring up at us, that Sharps still in her hand. I was all set to hit dirt if she swung that cannon up but she didn't. Instead, she sat down on the front steps and buried her face in her hands.

I went over and sat down beside her, slipping an arm around them strong shoulders of hers.

"I have taken life. I dedicated my own to bringing life into the world and giving new life a good start," she said, and her eyes brimmed over.

"He was fixing to kill you, Maud. He was escaping the noose, too. Ten or twelve men, women, and children he killed whilst robbing them."

"Why did it have to be me?"

"Because you were protecting Caroline and yourself and the new life she's carrying," I said, soft as I could.

She looked up. "Oh! Mr. Padlock. I'm so glad to see you're safe. And you too, Mr. Coop."

The sun warmed the steps. Maud and Caroline and I sat there watching Win and Padlock haul Strunck off somewhere.

"We're safe, Maud. Them of us still left. But we have to get on up to White Sulphur fast. You're about to get yourself a new brand, the one on your calves, and we've got to get it into the Montana Brand Book pronto. And I've got some other business there, some business that's been overdue a long time."

277

CHAPTER 20

The next day Win kindly fetched my buggy from the roundup camp for me, and by afternoon Maud and me were driving to White Sulphur. Padlock and Win and Caroline stayed on at the Fishhook to look after things.

When Padlock started to gather up what was left of Jerome I asked him to hold off on the burying until I got back, because I wanted to pay my respects.

"We plant our dead in a tree," he said. "It is the Blackfeet way."

"I'm sorry you lost him."

The Indian stared at me. "He is in the Sand Hills now, the place where our people go. He died bravely. It is perhaps better there than living in a white man's world."

I couldn't think of anything to say.

"Still," Padlock said, "he wished to be a doctor. He had started to read Maud's medical library. He thought that with that, and his share from the ranch, he might manage, and then take your scientific medicine to our people."

"I'm more sorry than I can say."

He gazed with those expressionless black eyes. "Go do your business in White Sulphur, Sheriff Oglesby." He smiled.

We drove all afternoon and into the evening, me and Maud, and when we got to town we slipped through the dark to Francis Harp's. I knew what I wanted to do but I didn't have enough law in my head to figger how. He sure beamed when we entered his parlor, and in a moment he had the lamps turned up. It took a heap of talking to catch him up on all that had happened, but pretty soon it was told. And then I explained what I wanted to do.

"Do it in the morning," he said, "when Park's in his lair and Bark's in chambers. Don't go to their homes tonight. I'll handle the rest. We'll need a U.S. marshal and a special prosecutor from Helena."

I took Maud over to the Sherman Hotel and stared down Smoot so that he gave her a room without no backtalk.

In the morning I sponged off what was left of my black worsted suit, got into a clean white shirt and string tie, climbed into the suit, buckled on my six-gun, and combed my hair real good. My behind was so sore I could hardly sit but it made no difference. I shined the star some, breathed on it and polished it, and pinned it in its place. I checked my hand-cuffs and the loads in my six-gun as well.

Then I strode uptown, kind of jaunty, and barged right into Park's office.

"Where the hell have you been?" he snarled. "You got those Indians locked up? And where's Wall? She was supposed to be kept at the hotel."

"Clyde Park, you're under arrest," I said, and I rattled off a string of items that Francis Harp gave me to say.

"Are you crazy? You can't arrest a county attorney! Get out of here! Give me your star, you idiot; you're through!"

I slid my six-gun out a few seconds ahead of his own hand, which was sliding into his desk drawer, and he seen I was serious and glared pop-eyed at me as I slipped cuffs on and prodded him off to cell number one.

Then I whistled over to the courthouse and found Judge Bark in chambers. I must say, he was apoplectic. I recited them charges that Harp gave me, conspiracy for this and that, put cuffs on him, and prodded him out of there, still early in the morning. It would take a few hours before all them county officials got to wondering where he was. He was howling like a coyote on a winter's night, saying all sorts of uncomplimentary things about me and my mother, but I didn't pay never no mind – I told him to shut up or he'd have a headache. I stuffed him in cell number two.

Francis Harp had his trap pulled up behind the jailhouse and we stuffed them two turkeys into it after I had tied rags over their blasphemous mouths. Then I added leg irons for good measure, drew the side curtains of that trap, and headed south like on some summer lark. I would deliver the goods to Deputy Coop at the Fishhook, and he would relay the goods to Sheriff Bo Svee in Livingston for safekeeping.

I tarried at the Fishhook long enough to pay my respects to Jerome. Padlock led me out to the place and I pinned a deputy badge on his shroud up in the tree.

Well, it all turned out fine. The territorial prosecutor, Curtis Wallman, got testimony from Maud and Padlock and Caroline and Harp and Ormly Richard and Bo Svee and Win Coop and me and those NP people and some of the square drovers. And he looked over a heap of evidence: the partnership papers, the will, the marriage certificate, Ham Bark's sales sheet for fifty Fishhook steers, a mess of trumped up warrants and court orders over the signatures of Park and Bark. And he came on out and looked at a few longhorn calves with that odd brand on them. Then he swung into action and pretty soon the courts had packed Dan Monk, Clyde Park, and Jeff Bark off to Deer Lodge. As for the rest of them stockmen, he invited them to a little meeting in the courthouse and showed them a list of charges on each of them as long as his arm and told them that the charges wouldn't expire for three years and if they so much as blew their noses too noisy he'd throw the book at them. They all tippytoed out like reformed fallen doves.

Maud set up at the Fishhook and it soon was a lively, happy place with lots of unfortunate women finding a chance to live again – and Padlock, who owned two-thirds of it, tending the stock and spinning Blackfeet stories for the young ladies and bringing a few Blackfeet women in to help and to learn midwifing.

Me, I won that election. I don't know how it happened. I figgered I was done for as sheriff, but Maxfield Perkins had printed the whole story in the newspaper and was saying lots of nice things about me, and I guess that put me in again.

I got a telegram from some jasper claiming to be Ned Buntline in New York. He wanted to write up my story and was full of hot air about me being "the very essence of the western lawman."

I thought about it some, and wired that jasper that I wasn't interested. I figgered I didn't fit the bill. Instead of being lean and handsome, I had a pot that wouldn't quit. Instead of being brave and stoic, I sobbed like a colicky baby when I was about to be executed. Instead of riding saddle and camping on bare ground as if I was born to it, I took to buggies and soft seats and cots and mattresses and tents. Instead of being some cool deadshot and a fast draw, I hated even to wear that heavy iron on my hip. It made me uncomfortable. I will say, though, I did earn the right to wear that shiny star, and that felt good. Perkins donated money for a silver one, and I wore it proud.